"I realize you ... spent the night with a man before."

Hank saw the flush coloring Angela's cheeks. "And what makes you think I haven't had a lover…or a dozen lovers? You think no man would find me desirable?"

"No, that's not it at all," Hank interjected, surprised at her instantaneous fury. "It has nothing to do with the way you look. I…there's an innocence about you. I just thought probably you were rather inexperienced."

"It's smarter to ask than to assume," she said stiffly.

He hesitated a moment, knowing he shouldn't, but unable to stop himself. "So, how many lovers have you had?"

"That, Hank Riverton, is none of your business. And now I believe I'll go to bed." Without turning back, she left the patio.

Hank stared after Angela. He had a feeling there was a lot more to his secretary than met the eye.…

***

Look for Carla Cassidy's next Silhouette Romance novel in January 2000.
The Princess's White Knight (#1415)
is part of Silhouette's exciting new cross-line continuity ROYALLY WED.

Dear Reader,

Silhouette Romance blends classic themes and the challenges of romance in today's world into a reassuring, fulfilling novel. And this month's offerings undeniably deliver on that promise!

In *Baby, You're Mine*, part of BUNDLES OF JOY, RITA Award-winning author Lindsay Longford tells of a pregnant, penniless widow who finds sanctuary with a sought-after bachelor who'd never thought himself the marrying kind…until now. Duty and passion collide in Sally Carleen's *The Prince's Heir*, when the prince dispatched to claim his nephew falls for the heir's beautiful adoptive mother. When a single mom desperate to keep her daughter weds an ornery rancher intent on saving his spread, she discovers that *McKenna's Bartered Bride* is what she wants to be…forever. Don't miss this next delightful installment of Sandra Steffen's BACHELOR GULCH series.

Donna Clayton delivers an emotional story about the bond of sisterhood…and how a career-driven woman learns a valuable lesson about love from the man who's *Her Dream Come True*. Carla Cassidy's MUSTANG, MONTANA, Intimate Moments series crosses into Romance with a classic boss/secretary story that starts with the proposition *Wife for a Week*, but ends…well, you'll have to read it to find out! And in Pamela Ingrahm's debut Romance novel, a millionaire CEO realizes that his temporary assistant—and her adorable toddler—have him yearning to leave his *Bachelor Boss* days behind.

Enjoy this month's titles—and keep coming back to Romance, a series guaranteed to touch *every* woman's heart.

Mary-Theresa Hussey

Mary-Theresa Hussey
Senior Editor

Please address questions and book requests to:
Silhouette Reader Service
U.S.: 3010 Walden Ave., P.O. Box 1325, Buffalo, NY 14269
Canadian: P.O. Box 609, Fort Erie, Ont. L2A 5X3

WIFE FOR
A WEEK

Carla Cassidy

Silhouette
R O M A N C E™
Published by Silhouette Books
America's Publisher of Contemporary Romance

To Angela Ulrich, the "daughter"
who likes to borrow my clothes!
Stay true and strong,
because I love you.

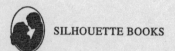 SILHOUETTE BOOKS

ISBN 0-373-19400-5

WIFE FOR A WEEK

Copyright © 1999 by Carla Bracale

Visit us at www.romance.net

Printed in U.S.A.

CARLA CASSIDY

is an award-winning author who has written thirty-five books for Silhouette. In 1995 she won Best Silhouette Romance of 1995 from *Romantic Times Magazine* for her Silhouette Romance novel *Anything for Danny*. In 1998 she also won a Career Achievement Award for Best Innovative Series from *Romantic Times Magazine*.

Carla believes the only thing better than curling up with a good book to read is sitting down at the computer with a good story to write. She's looking forward to writing many more books and bringing hours of pleasure to readers.

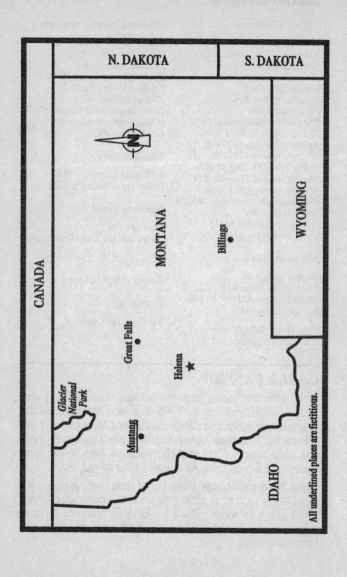

Chapter One

"I need a wife."

Angela Samuels stared at her boss, wondering if perhaps she'd misunderstood his words. Maybe he'd told her to "get a life." Heaven knows she could use one, but no, that couldn't have been what he said. Hank Riverton of Riverton Advertising Enterprises had never paid enough attention to her to know whether she had a life or not.

"I beg your pardon?" she finally said as she tightened her grip on her memo pad and pencil.

Hank Riverton leaned forward, his dark blue eyes studying her...assessing her. She felt the warmth of a blush stain her cheeks as his gaze traveled the length of her, starting at her head where she knew her long brown curly hair had probably partially escaped the clasp at the nape of her neck, down to the tip of her sensible, but ugly black shoes.

He nodded, as if satisfied with what he saw. "You'll do just fine. Of course it will only be a temporary, pretend kind of thing. One week. That's all I need from you."

"Mr. Riverton, I really don't know what you're talking about," she exclaimed.

He frowned, the gesture doing nothing to detract from his attractiveness. "Didn't we talk about this before? About Brody Robinson and his wife's marriage encounter retreat?"

Angela shook her head. Hank sighed and raked a hand through his thick dark hair. "I thought I mentioned something about this yesterday."

Again Angela shook her head. "Not to me." There was no way she would have forgotten a conversation where the topic was her becoming her boss's temporary wife.

"You know Brody Robinson?"

"Of Brody's Biscuits," Angela replied. Robinson was the largest account Hank's firm handled. Brody was a colorful pseudocowboy who'd made a fortune by packaging his grandmother's biscuit recipe in a ready-to-heat-and-eat format.

"He recently bought a ranch out in Mustang, Montana, and my 'wife' and I have been invited to go. When I landed the account last year, Brody got the idea that I was married."

Angela looked at him in surprise. Hank Riverton was the most unmarried man Angela had ever met. "How on earth did he get that impression?" she asked.

Hank cast her a slightly sheepish grin. "He just assumed I was married by the way I was talking and I didn't do anything to correct the assumption." The smile fell away and he frowned once again. "Hell, Angela, you know Brody. We won the biscuit account with an ad campaign based on family, home and good old-fashioned values. Brody is the most conservative man I know and he assumes I'm a kindred spirit."

Angela swallowed a burst of laughter. Hank Riverton, conservative? Hardly! Especially when it came to his personal life and relationships. She had a feeling his bedroom probably had a revolving door installed for convenience's sake. "What's this marriage encounter thing?" she asked.

Hank leaned back in his chair. "Brody's wife is a psychologist who specializes in saving marriages. She's developed a week-long program geared to deepening commitment and intimacy between married people." He said "commitment" and "intimacy" as if they were both four-letter words. "Anyway, Brody thought it would be a terrific gift to give me and my 'wife' a week at his ranch in Mustang, where his wife conducts these seminars. So, next Monday afternoon I'll be in Mustang, and if I'm without a wife, I'm fairly certain there's a strong possibility that Brody will pull his account."

"What about Sheila?" Angela replied, referring to Hank's latest love of his life.

He stared at her in disbelief. "Think about it,

Angela," he said dryly. "Does Sheila really come across as wife material?"

No. The flaming redhead with the dynamite figure she revealed more than covered definitely didn't give the impression of wifely attributes.

Rather Angela thought the sexy woman probably made men think of hot nights and steamy, illicit sex. Definitely mistress material rather than the substance of a wife.

"You, on the other hand, are perfect," Hank continued. Angela didn't know whether to feel complimented or insulted. "Look, it's just a week. It will be like a vacation." He leaned forward once again, his dark eyes holding a bewitching appeal.

Angela wondered if it was the same kind of look he gave when he was attempting to bed a woman. It was the first time she'd ever had those sexy eyes completely trained on her, and warmth started at her toes and slowly worked to suffuse her entire body.

"I just don't think this is a good idea," she murmured, gripping her memo pad against her chest. "What if I say something wrong? Jeopardize the account?" she hedged. "The whole idea is crazy."

"You're right," he agreed easily. "The whole idea is crazy, but I've got to do it and I need you in order to pull it off. One week," he hesitated, then added, "and I'll give you a bonus of a thousand dollars."

Angela widened her eyes at the incentive. What she couldn't do with a thousand dollars. Her mother needed a new air-conditioning unit and her brother, Brian, always needed extra money for school. And if she intended to hunt for a new job, the money would afford her a little time to decide exactly what she wanted to do.

"Fifteen hundred," Hank said. "For a week that will be more vacation than work."

"Okay," Angela reluctantly agreed, knowing it was probably a mistake, but unable to turn down a windfall that would ease her family's financial situation at least for a little while.

"Terrific!" Hank stood, a smile of relief curving his lips. "Why don't you take the rest of the afternoon off, go home and write up a sort of dossier on yourself. Bring it to work in the morning and that will give me all weekend to study it. I'll write up the same for you. By Monday we need to know enough about each other so we can give the impression that we've been married for some time."

Angela knew she was dismissed when he sat down and opened a manila folder. She left his office and walked out to the reception area where her own desk awaited her.

Although she had been working for Hank Riverton for the past two years, she wasn't sure she intended to keep the job much longer. When he had first interviewed her for the job, he'd explained to her that her position would include the duties of a personal assistant as well as that of secretary.

Angela had been thrilled to get the job in the one-man office and at first hadn't minded running his personal errands, buying his aunt and his father their birthday presents and picking up his dry cleaning. She hoped that eventually she'd work up to her dream of copywriting, of actually being a part of the creative process involved in advertising.

In the initial interview Hank had mentioned the possibility of advancement and knowing the Riverton Advertising Agency's reputation in the business, she was thrilled with the opportunity to learn from him.

So far she'd learned he liked his shirts starched heavy and his sandwiches without mayo. She'd discovered his average dating time for any one woman was about three weeks and he always sent flowers when he dumped them. Although she felt she'd learned much in the past two years, she'd had no way of putting her knowledge to use. She felt stymied and wasted and wanted more from her job.

She quickly cleared off the top of her desk, but paused at the large picture of her boss that graced the wall opposite her.

Hank Riverton. At the age of thirty-three he was already highly successful in the advertising business despite his relative youth and the fact the he worked neither on the east coast or the west, but instead out of Great Falls, Montana.

He was a hunk, no question about it. His dark hair was thick and wavy, his eyes midnight-blue. His chiseled features not only radiated attractiveness, but intelligence as well.

For the first couple of months she'd worked for

him, Angela had entertained a massive crush on him. She'd been tongue-tied in his presence, her heart had quickened when he was near and she'd suffered erotic dreams about him nearly every night.

The crush had waned, leaving behind an admiration for his business sense, but the knowledge that he was certainly not the kind of man she'd want to fall in love with. She admired his business acumen, but wasn't even sure she liked him very much.

With a deep sigh, she grabbed her purse and left the office. As she drove home, the reality of what she'd just agreed to set in.

Wife for a week. Hank Riverton's wife for a week. Rolling down the window, she breathed deeply of the warm, late summer air and fought the impulse to turn the car around and tell Mr. Riverton that she wouldn't be a party to the lie he intended to perpetrate.

What's more, she wanted to tell him that she was tired of being a gofer for a man who rarely acknowledged her existence as a real, living, breathing person.

The idea of pretending to be his wife for a week was total lunacy. The idea of collecting fifteen hundred dollars for the moment of insanity was frighteningly comforting.

It isn't fair to perpetuate a lie, take money for doing it, then quit the job, a little voice whispered in her head. Do the week, take the money, then run, a louder voice exclaimed.

Angela decided to listen to the big-mouth. After all, the lie was relatively harmless and the money had been offered as a bonus.

After the week was up if she decided to quit the job, she'd give Hank Riverton the required two weeks' notice. She owed him nothing beyond that.

As she turned into the driveway of her mother's small house, she wondered how to explain the trip to her mom. A business trip, that's all she had to say.

She didn't have to mention the little part about pretending to be Hank's wife. She knew her mother wouldn't approve of such a deception. Besides, Angela was twenty-eight years old...old enough to have a few secrets from her mother.

As she got out of the car, her mind quickly jumped to the next problem at hand. What did one pack for a week of "pretend wife" at a Montana ranch?

"Yes, Brody. We're really looking forward to it," Hank said into the receiver. "We're driving in and planning on arriving around noon tomorrow."

"Great, great!" Brody Robinson's deep voice boomed across the line. "You'll love Mustang and I guarantee you and the Mrs. will come away from here feeling like newlyweds."

"Angela and I can't wait," Hank replied.

"Angela?" Brody paused a moment. "I thought your wife's name was Marie."

Hank felt the blood leave his head. Of course, at

the time he'd landed the Robinson account he'd been dating Marie. "Angela Marie," he improvised. "I call her by both names."

"Must get damn confusing," Brody replied. "Oh well, I don't care what you call her as long as you bring her along. We've invited two other couples to join you. Should be a great week."

After a bit more small talk, the two men said goodbye. Hank leaned back on the sofa and drew a deep breath. He hated the deception he was about to pull, but he'd talked himself in a corner and didn't know any other way to get out.

He picked up the dossier Angela had given him on Friday. He hadn't had time to look at it until this moment, which gave him less than twenty-four hours to learn what he could about her.

Funny, she'd been working for him for almost two years and he didn't know anything about her personal life. Of course, he'd had no reason to care until now. She was highly efficient, nearly invisible as she accomplished all the tasks that made his business and personal life run smoothly.

He frowned, surprised to discover he couldn't bring a clear picture of her into his mind. He wasn't sure if her eyes were blue or brown, although he did recall that her hair was a nondescript brown and usually untidy.

Still, her features remained indistinct and the only other thing he could bring to mind about her was the fact that she always wore black ugly sensible shoes.

At least he wouldn't have to worry about somehow getting carried away in the role playing. His mousy secretary wasn't his type at all and that's what made her so perfect for the part.

With a sigh he got up and crossed the living room. He was not looking forward to the coming week. Seven days in a little cow town learning how to develop deeper intimacy wasn't his idea of a vacation.

Intimacy. What every woman longed for and what every man abhorred. Hank didn't want some woman inside his head, knowing his thoughts, sharing his dreams.

He'd seen what love and intimacy had done to his father. Hank's mother had died when Hank had been five, and for years Hank had watched his father build a dry-cleaning empire through long hours and hard work.

Then, a year ago Harris Riverton had remarried and had been transformed from a sharp businessman to a doddering old fool who loved nothing more than puttering in the garden with his new bride.

No way Hank ever wanted to lose his edge, share his energy, compromise his needs for any woman.

Speaking of women…he looked at his watch and stood. He was supposed to pick up Sheila in fifteen minutes for their customary Sunday night dinner together.

An hour later he and Sheila sat at a table in Sam's Steakhouse, Hank's favorite restaurant. The decor was uninspiring, the ambience unmemorable, but the steaks were huge and cooked to perfection.

As Hank dug into his rare T-bone, Sheila picked at a salad, her dainty features pulled into a frown of petulance. She'd been angry with him ever since he'd told her he'd be gone for the next week on business. She pouted until he'd almost finished his steak.

"Are you sure you can't get back to town in time for the fund-raiser on Friday night?" She finally broke the silence that had lingered between them.

"Sorry, honey. It's impossible. There's no way I can be back in town before next Sunday."

"But you're the boss. Can't you just make somebody else do whatever business it is that has to be done? The cocktail party is so important. Everyone who is anyone will be there." Sheila's normally buttery-smooth voice became a plaintive whine. "I was so looking forward to it. I bought a gorgeous new dress and I even managed to get a hair appointment with Pierre."

"You can still go to the party without me," Hank said, wondering why he'd never noticed before that Sheila's blue eyes had the cold, hard glare of a woman who liked to get her own way.

"Mustang is only a couple of hours away. You could drive in for the party, then drive back for business early on Saturday morning," she pressed, the hardness in her eyes deepening.

Hank set his fork down and shoved his plate aside. "Sheila, I'm sorry, I said I can't make it and

I mean it. There will always be another fund-raiser, another cocktail party.''

Sheila took a sip of her wine, her red lipstick staining the rim of the glass. She set the glass down then reached across the table for Hank's hand. ''What is little Sheila going to do for a whole week without her lover-bear?''

Hank hated it when she talked baby talk and he suddenly realized there was little about Sheila he really liked.

Granted, the woman had a dynamite face and figure, but she was also spoiled and demanding. They had very little in common with each other and he had a feeling Sheila liked him more for his image and the challenge he presented than anything else.

It was time to call an end to the three-week dating frenzy he'd shared with the attractive woman. As the thought crossed his mind, relief flowed through him, confirming that it was definitely time to end it.

He wiped his mouth with his napkin, struggling to find the right words without hurting her feelings or her dignity. ''Sheila, you're a nice, beautiful woman and I've really enjoyed the time we've spent together,'' he began.

''You're kissing me off, aren't you?'' Gone was the buttery tone as well as the baby talk. Instead her voice radiated anger. ''I can't believe this. All my friends warned me about you, Hank Riverton. They told me not to date you. They said that you are a professional heartbreaker.''

"Sheila..." Hank winced, but the woman continued.

"You just wait, Hank." She pushed back from the table and stood, looking more beautiful than ever with her ample chest heaving and her blue eyes flashing.

"One of these days you're going to give your heart to some woman. You're going to love her more than anything on earth, and I hope she takes your heart and smashes it to little pieces." With these words she whirled around and stomped away from the table.

Hank fought down a surge of regret as he watched the sexy sway of her backside in retreat. He imagined Sheila was probably a good lover, but he hadn't experienced her expertise in that particular area.

Although she had given him all the right signals nearly every night that they'd gone out, he hadn't responded. He knew Sheila would see lovemaking as a prelude to a wedding band, and that's the last thing Hank wanted. Besides, it was difficult to picture making love to a woman who baby-talked.

He was also sorry if he'd hurt her, although he knew Sheila would be fine with or without him. She was one of those women who would always have a man at her side. Like him, she was a survivor in the game of relationships.

He shoved any lingering regrets aside and waved to the waiter for his check. "Goodbye Sheila," he murmured to himself, somehow relieved that there would be no more dates with her.

Besides, it seemed fitting that he'd broken up with Sheila tonight. After all, first thing in the morning he would be a "married man."

As he waited for the waiter to return with his check, he thought of his secretary, the woman to play his wife. Angela was exactly the kind of woman Brody would approve of. Rather plain and quiet, dutiful and efficient, she had all the qualities of an old-fashioned, traditional wife. And best of all, she was definitely no threat to Hank's bachelorhood.

He smiled as he thought of Sheila's parting words. She hoped some woman broke his heart. He laughed aloud at the very thought. The day he allowed a woman access to his heart was the day he'd kiss Brody Robinson's ugly mug. Not in this lifetime, he promised himself.

Chapter Two

"Brian, stop!" Angela tried to muster a stern look, but instead dissolved into laughter as her brother held her hairbrush over his head. "Come on, I need to brush my hair before Mr. Riverton arrives."

Brian danced around her, holding out the brush, then snatching it away before she could grab it. He retreated behind the kitchen table, a grin on his thin face.

At nineteen, Brian was tall and gangly, still more boy than man with a wicked sense of humor that often made Angela half-crazy. "Why should I give it to you? You're just going to pull your hair back in one of those ugly barrettes," he exclaimed.

"My barrettes aren't ugly and my boss is going to be here any minute!" Angela raced around the table, playfully smacked her brother in the chest, then giggled once again as he wrapped her in a bear hug.

How she loved her baby brother, she thought as she struggled to get free of his embrace. Although Brian wasn't a baby any longer, he still held her heart.

Their father had walked out on them when their mother was pregnant with Brian and Angela had been nine. Soon after his abandonment and Brian's birth, their mother had developed a heart condition and it had been Angela who had done most of the raising of her baby brother. The result was a loving, close bond between the two siblings.

The doorbell rang and Angela froze, her heart thudded to a near halt in her chest. As she heard her mother answer the door, she struggled to get free from her bratty brother's hold. "If you don't let me go this minute, I'll…I'll…"

Brian laughed. "You'll what? I'm far too big for you to spank." He released her as Hank Riverton stepped into the kitchen.

"Good morning," Hank said, a dark eyebrow arched in surprise.

The heat of a blush swept over Angela as she snatched the brush from Brian's hand and swept her errant hair away from her face. "Good morning," she replied. "Uh…I'll be ready to go in just a moment. Brian, why don't you pour Mr. Riverton a cup of coffee."

"I'll take care of Mr. Riverton, you go ahead and

finish getting ready," Janette Samuels said as she entered the kitchen.

Angela flashed a smile of gratitude to her mother, then raced for her bedroom, where her suitcase was packed and waiting.

She quickly pulled her hair back and clasped it at the nape of her neck with a wide barrette. She didn't want to take too long. She didn't want her mother grilling Mr. Riverton about their "business trip."

She glanced at her reflection in her dresser mirror. Hank had told her casual dress and she'd taken him at his word. She wore jeans and a navy-and-white pullover blouse. Instead of her usual working shoes, white tennis shoes adorned her feet. After one last nervous glance in the mirror, she grabbed her suitcase and left her bedroom.

Her boss sat at the kitchen table, flanked by her mother and her brother. Brian was telling Hank about the classes he was taking at the local community college.

As Brian talked, Angela took a moment to study the man who would be her pretend husband for the next seven days. Clad in tight jeans and a short-sleeved polo shirt that emphasized his broad shoulders and biceps, he looked far too masculine, far too virile for comfort.

"Sounds like a tough schedule," Hank commented when Brian finished talking.

Angela walked from the doorway to stand behind her brother. She placed her hands on his shoulders.

"Brian can handle it. He was valedictorian of his high school and had scholarship offers from colleges all around the country." Her voice rang with her pride.

Janette patted her son's hand. "And next year he'll be at one of those colleges instead of at the community college here in town."

"We'll see, Mom," Brian replied noncommittedly.

Hank stood and looked at Angela expectantly. "We've got quite a drive ahead of us. We'd better get on the road."

"Yes, of course." Angela picked up her suitcase and started toward the front door.

"Here, let me." He took the suitcase from her, then turned to her mother. "It was a pleasure meeting you, Mrs. Samuels. I'll take good care of your daughter and deliver her home safe and sound next Sunday."

Angela's mother smiled. "That's fine. I hope your business goes well."

"Bye, sis," Brian said.

"Bye, Brian. Don't you skip any classes while I'm gone," Angela exclaimed.

She breathed a sigh of relief as they stepped out of the house and into the cool early morning air. Hank stowed her suitcase in the trunk as she got into the passenger seat of the bright red, two-seater sports car.

"Sorry I wasn't ready when you arrived. I didn't mean for you to have to cool your heels with my mom and brother," she said nervously as he slid in behind the wheel.

"I didn't mind," he said. He started the car with a roar, then turned and looked at her. "In fact, I found it rather interesting. Over the weekend as I read the dossier you prepared, I realized I knew absolutely nothing about you." He pulled away from the curb.

"There isn't much to know," she said.

"On the contrary. I had no idea you had any family. You're always available to work long hours and on the weekends. If I remember correctly you supervised a party at my place nearly all night last Christmas Eve."

Angela shrugged. "It's not like I have a husband or children. Both Mom and Brian know how important my job is to me." She battled with herself, wondering if this was the moment to tell him how unhappy she'd been with what her job had become. She decided now wasn't the time. Perhaps on the drive home after the week was over.

For a few minutes they rode in silence, fighting the morning rush-hour traffic as they headed out of town. He was a skillful driver, weaving in and out of other cars in an attempt to minimize their travel time.

She cast him a surreptitious glance, realizing perhaps the crush she'd once had on him wasn't completely gone. Although she knew he was a playboy, seemingly unable to sustain any long-term relationships, she couldn't help but be affected by his nearness. And it irritated her.

Something about him reminded her of her own femininity, the sexuality that had yet to be awakened. Twenty-eight-years old and never been kissed.

Oh, sure there had been a little bit of dating and kissing in high school, but the reality of her mother's illness and Brian's needs as a growing boy had made relationships impossible for Angela.

She was sweet twenty-eight and had never felt the thrill, the utter turn-on of a kiss from an adult, experienced male. And something about Hank Riverton reminded her of her inadequacies and inexperience.

"So, why is your brother going to a community college if he had so many other offers?" he asked as he hit the highway that would take them to Mustang.

Angela pulled herself from her reverie, grateful for any conversation that would still her disturbing thoughts. "At the time the offers came in, my mother was going through a rough time. She has a heart condition and we weren't sure she was going to make it through the crisis. Brian decided he'd rather stay close to home."

"That's commendable. What about your father? What does he do?"

"Who knows?" Angela fought down the anger and hurt, thoughts of her father always brought. "He walked out on us when Mom was pregnant with Brian. He decided not to leave a forwarding address.''

"Ouch," Hank winced. "Well, that's one thing we have in common. We both came from single-parent homes. My mother died when I was five."

"Yes, I know," Angela replied. He looked at her in surprise and she continued. "Before I interviewed for you, I did some homework. I read every newspaper and magazine article I could get my hands on about you." She didn't mention that it was at this time she'd developed her crush on him.

He cast her a rueful smile. "I certainly hope you don't believe everything you've read. Writers tend to exaggerate, especially when it comes to making money and making love."

Angela blushed, but held his gaze. "I've worked for you long enough to know that you seem to do both very well."

He laughed. "Depends on who you ask. According to my accountant, I spend nearly as much as I make, and I have a feeling if you'd ask Sheila what she thought about me today, she wouldn't have much glowing praise."

"Trouble in paradise?" she asked.

"Paradise lost," he replied. "I broke it off with her last night."

"Should I call the florist?" she asked teasingly.

"Nah, we'll skip the normal routine. Besides, it just wouldn't seem right, sending Sheila flowers when I'm married to you." He grinned and Angela felt the magnetism of his smile zing throughout her body. "And speaking of us being married, we need to discuss some of the details of our wedding."

"Like what?" she asked.

"Like were we married in a traditional ceremony or in a park or at a justice of the peace? Did we have a long courtship or a whirlwind romance?"

"Definitely a whirlwind romance," she replied after a moment of thought. "But we married in a traditional ceremony." She closed her eyes for a moment, instantly able to visualize the wedding she'd always dreamed of. "We had an evening ceremony, with lots of candles lit and arrangements of baby's breath and orange blossoms. I wore a long white gown with tiny pearl seed buttons and a train of lace. You wore a black tuxedo with a pale pink cummerbund and bow tie."

"Sounds like you've given this a lot of thought."

His voice jerked her from the pleasant image, the result as startling and frustrating as awakening in the middle of a pleasant dream. "Not really," she said, not wanting him to know how often she entertained such ridiculous fantasies. "I suppose everyone at one time or another thinks about what they would want their wedding to be like."

"I can honestly say that wedding thoughts have never crossed my mind."

Angela smiled dryly. "And I can honestly say that doesn't surprise me. You have the heart of a perpetual bachelor." She hesitated a moment, eyeing him curiously. "I'm not sure you can pull off the role of a married man for a whole week."

One of his dark brows rose and his deep blue eyes sparked with challenge. "Don't underestimate me, Angela. You've worked with me long enough to know that I'm ruthless when it comes to getting what I want and it's vitally important that Brody believes I'm happily married to you. Trust me…I'll perform my part. Are you certain you can do yours?"

She smiled at him with a show of confidence. "I've worked for you long enough that you should know I'm nothing if not highly efficient. If you require me to act as your wife, then that's exactly what I will do."

Hank laughed, the deep, robust sound reverberating pleasantly in the pit of Angela's stomach. "I have a feeling this might just prove to be a very interesting week."

His laughter combined with the challenge in his eyes, and created a ball of heat in the pit of Angela's stomach. She realized at that moment she'd made a huge mistake in agreeing to the whole madcap scheme.

For the next hour they fabricated their life together, deciding they'd honeymooned in the Caribbean, had vacationed in New York City, and on most Friday nights played cards with several other young couples. When they felt as if all bases had been covered, they fell into an easy silence.

As the surrounding landscape grew monotonous, Angela leaned her head against the side window and within minutes appeared to be asleep. Hank took the opportunity to study her.

She'd surprised him. When he'd arrived to pick her up and he'd first spied her in her brother's grip, her hair wild and curly and flowing around her shoulders, it had been like seeing a stranger for the first time.

Had her hair always been that long, that thick and shiny? Why had he never noticed it before?

It wasn't just the sight of her hair that had shocked him. As they'd talked, she'd surprised him with her dry wit and a touch of spunk, humor and spirit she never exhibited at work.

He glanced at her, quickly taking in her features. She certainly wasn't a raving beauty. In fact, she wasn't even that pretty. Her hair was a nonremarkable brown, pulled back and contained in a barrette as was her usual fashion. Her chin was a little too sharp, her nose a trifle too long. At a time when thick lips were a hot commodity, Angela's were thin and not particularly welcoming.

He focused back on the road, pleased that at least he didn't have to worry about being physically attracted to her. The week would have been pure hell had he been pretending to be married to a knockout.

He congratulated himself on his inspired choice. Asking his plain-Jane secretary to play the role had been a stoke of genius on his part. There was no chance that either of them would take the game too seriously.

When they were just a few miles outside of Mustang, Angela stirred and opened her eyes.

"Hey sleepyhead," Hank greeted her. "We'll be in Mustang in about ten minutes."

She straightened. "Oh, I'm sorry. I didn't mean to fall asleep." Her hands shot to her hair in a gesture of self-consciousness. "Riding in a car always does that to me."

"Don't worry about it. There's one more little piece of business we need to take care of before we get there," he said as he reached into his pocket. He pulled out a jeweler's box and handed it to her.

"What's this?" she asked.

"Your wedding ring, of course."

She snapped open the lid and gasped. "Oh, it's beautiful."

Hank nodded. "It was my mother's ring. I figured you wearing it would be a nice touch. Put it on."

She slid the ring on her finger. "It's a little big, but it will be fine. I promise I'll take very good care of it for this week."

He smiled at her. "I guess now it's official. You're wearing my ring, so that makes you my girl."

"You know this is crazy," she said as she studied the ring with its large center diamond and spray of smaller ones in a flower design.

"What's crazy is if I allow Brody Robinson to take his account elsewhere." He fell silent as they

entered the Mustang city limits and he tried to remember the directions Brody had given him.

"What a charming little town," Angela exclaimed as they drove down Main Street.

Hank nodded, following her gaze toward the old,
but attractive storefronts, the tree-lined sidewalks
and the remains of a different era that endured in
the form of hitching posts.

"Brody's place is on the other side of town, several miles to the west," he explained. "Getting nervous?" he asked as she fidgeted in the seat next to
him.

"A little," she replied, then smiled. "I've never
been married before."

Her smile did something to her face...lit it up,
detracted from the irregular features and emphasized the shine of her eyes and her perfect straight
white teeth. Her smile almost made her pretty.

"This is as close as I ever intend to get to the
matrimony state," he said, his voice ringing more
forcefully than he intended.

It took only minutes for them to drive through
the small town. When they reached the other side,
Hank spied his turnoff, a gravel two-lane road that
would take them to Brody's place.

Even without the large sign that read Robinson's
Ranch, Hank would have known the place belonged
to his client by the huge wrought iron biscuit that
set atop the gate.

"There's nothing subtle about Brody," he murmured as the ranch house came into view.

"My goodness. It's a mansion," Angela exclaimed.

Indeed it was a mansion. The house was a two-story structure of mammoth proportions. Above the wrapping veranda with its massive columns, two balconies protruded out from the second floor.

In the distance a series of outbuildings could be seen along with hundreds of jersey cows dotting the seemingly never-ending pasture.

"Quite impressive," Hank said as he pulled the car to a halt in front of the main house. "Brody never does anything halfway." He turned off the engine and at that moment Brody Robinson barreled out the front door and toward them. Hank turned and grinned at Angela, who looked tense. "We're on," he said softly. "Act married."

Brody yanked open Hank's car door. "Hank, it's good to see you." The big, burly cowboy half hauled Hank from the car, then raced around to help Angela out. "And you must be the little lady," he exclaimed as he wrapped Angela in a bear hug. "Come on in and meet my better half. Don't worry about the bags. I'll have one of the hands bring them in."

As Brody lead them from the car, Hank took Angela's hand in his. Cold. Like ice. He flashed her a reassuring smile. She returned him a tentative one.

"Barbara," Brody bellowed as they walked through the front door and into a huge entryway. "The first of our guests have arrived."

He grinned at Hank and Angela. "The other couples will be here later this evening." They all turned at the sound of approaching heels against the marble floor. "Ah, here's my bride now."

Tall and slender, attractive with short gray hair and vivid green eyes, Barbara Robinson exuded warmth and friendliness. Brody threw his big arm around her shoulders and made the introductions. "This is Hank, the mastermind behind our ad campaign, and his lovely wife, who he sometimes calls Marie and sometimes calls Angela."

"Please, make it Angela," Angela said as she accepted the hand Barbara offered. "And thank you for inviting us into your home. Hank and I have been looking forward to being here."

Hank felt a swell of pride. Angela sounded gracious and sincere, two qualities he'd want in a wife...if he wanted a wife.

"Please, come into the living room. I've just made some fresh lemonade. We'll visit a little bit before we get you settled into your room." Barbara led them into the large living room and gestured toward the sofa. "I'll be right back with the refreshments."

As Barbara left the room, Hank sat on the sofa, Angela by his side. Brody sank into an overstuffed chair across from them. "You came through Mustang?" he asked.

Hank nodded. "Nice little town."

"Best damn town in the whole United States," Brody exclaimed. "Best damn people in the whole world. Barbara and I love it here. We've only been here a couple of months, but wouldn't consider living anywhere else on earth." He grinned at the two of them. "You two make such a fine couple. How long have you been married?"

"Two years next month," Angela said. Hank nodded, pleased that Angela was obviously a quick study.

"Ah, so you had a summer wedding." Brody smiled. "Barbara and I got married in December in the middle of the worst blizzard in Montana history. I near froze to death getting to the church, but being married to her has kept me warm ever since."

"He's a sentimental old fool," Barbara said as she entered the room carrying a tray of drinks. She smiled fondly at her husband. "Every time it snows he wants to renew our vows…and it snows a lot in Montana."

She handed them each a glass of lemonade, then sat down in the chair next to where her husband sat. "Do you work, Angela?" she asked.

"It's a full-time job keeping Hank's life running smoothly so he can concentrate his energies on the business." She laid a hand on his arm. "I just don't know what he'd do without me."

"I'm sure he feels the same way," Brody exclaimed.

Hank smiled, although he thought Angela was laying it on a little thick. He sipped his lemonade, watching his "wife" as she and Barbara exchanged small talk.

She was right, he finally admitted to himself. He

didn't know what he'd do without her. Although he rarely took notice of her at work, it was because she kept things running so smoothly he didn't have to take notice.

She kept his appointments straight, ordered gifts for friends and relatives. She always seemed to know the names of clients' children and spouses, and the important little things that enhanced whatever business he was conducting.

He'd had half a dozen secretaries before her, attractive women who seemed more content filing their nails than papers. Yes, he didn't know what he would do without Angela, and he hoped he never had to find out. He didn't need a wife, but he definitely needed a good secretary.

"The first five years, those are the hardest in a marriage," Brody said to Hank, pulling Hank from his thoughts. "If you can weather those years, then you'll grow stronger, better together." He smiled at his wife, and in his eyes Hank saw lasting love and enduring commitment. "Barbara and I are getting ready to celebrate our thirtieth wedding anniversary."

"That's quite an accomplishment," Hank said, truly impressed. Thirty years with the same woman. Hank couldn't imagine thirty days.

"We've weathered many a storm together, but each trial and tribulation only made us stronger," Brody exclaimed. He smiled at his wife. "Nothing better for a man than a woman who loves him...and nothing better for a woman than a man who loves her."

"If we don't stop him now, Brody will wax poetic for hours," Barbara said with a laugh. "And I'm sure you two would like to get settled in and freshen up a bit before dinner," Barbara said. "Brody, why don't you take them upstairs, dear, and I'll just take the glasses back in to the kitchen."

Barbara collected their lemonade glasses then Angela and Hank followed Brody out of the living room and up the massive staircase.

"You have a beautiful home, Mr. Robinson," Angela said.

"Thank you, honey, we've put a lot of work into it since we bought it…and please, make it Brody," the big cowboy said as they reached the top of the stairs. He turned into the first room on the left. "We're putting you two in here."

Angela and Hank followed him into the attractive, airy bedroom. The pale white carpeting was plush, complementing the dark cherry wood furniture. "I'll just leave you two to get unpacked and settled in," Brody said. With a nod to them both he turned and left, his footsteps loud and heavy as he went back down the stairs.

Hank stared at the double bed, covered with an attractive mint green spread. A tiny double bed. Everything Brody did was big…Hank had assumed the beds would be big as well. He'd expected king-size. He'd expected something different than this.

He and Angela hadn't talked about the sleeping

arrangements. It was the one thing that hadn't been discussed about the week they'd be spending together.

He turned and looked at her, and he could tell by the look on her face that like him, she'd assumed the bed would be a king-size.

The only other piece of furniture in the room was a dainty love seat...far too dainty and small for Hank's tall frame. He'd be crippled for life if he tried to sleep there.

"We are not going to share that bed," she said softly. "Nobody in this house has to know we aren't sleeping in the same bed."

Hank nodded and once again eyed the love seat. He looked back at her. "I'll raise your bonus to seventeen fifty if I get the bed."

She stared at the love seat for a long moment, then directed her gaze back to him. "You've got a deal."

Hank forced a smile to his face, knowing somehow that this week was going to cost him a small fortune.

Chapter Three

It didn't take long to unpack their bags. Hank took the bottom two drawers of the dresser and the left-hand side of the closet.

Angela took the top two drawers and the right-hand side of the closet. It looked odd, and strangely intimate to see their clothes hanging together in the small space.

"It's a good thing you told me to pack casual things," she said as she placed a pair of jeans in the drawer.

"Why is that?"

"Because if this had been anything more formal, I wouldn't have been able to provide the kinds of clothes Hank Riverton's wife would wear."

He sat on the edge of the bed and grinned at her. "And what do you think my wife would wear?"

She shrugged, wishing he'd get off the bed, wishing he didn't look so darned attractive. The whole situation felt obscenely intimate, making her wish she'd never agreed to the whole scheme.

"Silk," she answered his question. "Definitely lots of silk, and chic suits and flowing gowns. I'm sure your wife would be the kind of woman who would know all the latest fashions and wear them with real panache."

"I'm glad you can imagine my wife so easily. I certainly can't imagine her." He stood and walked over to the window. "I've never had any desire for a wife and I certainly have never met any woman who's made me change my mind."

"What are you so afraid of?" The question left her mouth before she consciously formed the thought.

He turned and gazed at her, amusement lighting his eyes. "What a typical female thing to say. Just because I don't want to get married, you assume it's because I'm secretly afraid of commitment, or fear intimacy or some other such psychobabble junk."

"You're right. I was giving you the benefit of the doubt. The truth is probably that you're too darned selfish and self-centered to want to share yourself with anyone." Angela clapped a hand over her mouth, horrified by her outburst.

Hank stared at her for a long moment. One corner of his mouth lifted into a half smile. "That's probably the most honest assessment I've ever received of myself.''

"I'm sorry...you just made me angry.''

He held up a hand. "Please, don't ruin it by apologizing." His grin widened. "And you're a very astute judge of character. I am selfish and self-centered. I'm also driven and difficult, and all those add up to poor husband material.''

"If only Brody could hear you now."

"Thank goodness he can't." He gazed at her with speculation. "I suppose you're one of those misguided romantics, who will only feel completely fulfilled by joining your life with a man's.''

"On the contrary, I don't need a man to fulfill me.'' Angela had always believed her happiness was in her own hands. She wasn't waiting for a man to make her whole. "However, eventually I would like to share my life with somebody.''

She looked away from him, remembering all the nights she'd imagined lying in somebody's arms, feeling another's body heat against her own. Someday she wanted to share herself, her days and nights, her dreams and disillusionments, with a special man. "I would be okay alone for the rest of my life, but that wouldn't be my first choice.''

"Well, that's definitely my first choice," he replied.

Angela laughed. "Oh Hank, you're never alone. You move from one woman to the next with little downtime in between.''

He looked at her in surprise, his smile falling

away. "But I always feel alone." He frowned and raked a hand through his hair. "Let's go take a tour of this place." His impatient tone let her know she'd touched a nerve. "I'm sure Brody won't mind if we look around until it's time for dinner."

She nodded, eager to leave the small confines of the bedroom, a bedroom where Hank's presence seemed to shrink the space between the walls.

Besides, the conversation had unsettled her. She talked a good game, but in truth, the idea of giving her heart to another person scared her to death. She'd given it once and it had come back broken and scarred. She wouldn't be so willing to easily give her heart again.

They went down the stairs and outside, onto the large front porch. "What do you say? Left or right?" Hank asked, gesturing first one direction, then the other.

"Doesn't matter to me," Angela replied.

Hank grinned. "On the contrary, I always let my wife make the decisions."

She returned his smile with a shake of her head. "Only if the decisions being made are as innocuous as which direction to take for a walk, right?"

He laughed. "Why is it that you never display such a sharp wit at the office?"

"I guess I don't have time. You keep me pretty busy." She wanted to tell him he kept her busy running his personal life, that she wished he'd get a real wife to take over those duties so she could concentrate more fully on her career in advertising.

But she kept her mouth shut on that score, unwilling to start the long week on the wrong foot.

They took off walking toward the large wooden corral just outside the barn, where half a dozen horses danced and pranced, stirring the ground into small puffs of dirt.

"You like horses?" he asked as they both leaned against the wooden enclosure and watched the handsome animals.

"Sure, I guess. I mean, I don't know. I've never really been around them," she replied.

"I imagine Brody will have us riding like cowboys by the end of the week."

"You mentioned Brody bought this place not long ago?" Angela asked, trying not to notice how the sun stroked fiery highlights into Hank's dark hair.

"Yes. He picked up this place about three months ago. Seems there was some sort of scandal and the woman who owned it, Rachel Emery, wanted to get away from Mustang. Brody picked it up for a song and is now living his dream of being a rootin'-tootin' cowboy."

Angela laughed. "He seems very nice," she said as they left the corral and walked toward the barn.

"Brody is the best," Hank agreed. "He really is exactly the man our firm has promoted him as, a little old-fashioned, but a man of honor and morals."

Angela frowned, a rolling sensation in the pit of

her stomach. "It doesn't feel right. Our fooling him with this marriage scam."

"I know, but don't go getting all sanctimonious on me," Hank exclaimed. "We aren't hurting anyone and both of us profit from the arrangement. Brody will never know the difference, so no real harm, no foul."

Angela nodded. He was right. She'd agreed to this madness, and now wasn't the time for second thoughts.

"Come on," Hank said, taking her arm lightly. "It will be all right." His touch was warm, and the light in his dark-blue eyes made anything seem possible. He grinned, a devilish handsome smile. "Ever explored a barn?"

Angela sighed, wondering how any woman ever told Hank no. He had the charm of the wicked flowing in his veins and she had a feeling he could convince a woman the sky was green if it was what he wanted her to believe.

The interior of the barn was dimly lit and smelled of sweet hay, old leather and the heavier musk of animal. It wasn't an unpleasant scent, just different than anything Angela had ever experienced.

Hank took her through the huge structure, showing her the stalls for the horses, the bins filled with grain and the cribs for corn. Angela was amazed at his apparent knowledge about all the items and nooks and crannies the barn contained.

After they'd seen everything on the bottom floor, he pulled down a set of stairs and they climbed to the loft, where bales of hay were stacked neatly from floor to ceiling.

"I once got my butt beat for sneaking up to a loft to smoke a cigarette," he said as he sat on one of the stray bales of hay. "I was about eight at the time and my dad switched me good as he told me I could have burned down our entire barn."

Angela sank down on a bale nearby. "I didn't know you grew up on a ranch." She found it hard to imagine him anywhere but in the city, the blood in his veins throbbing to the frantic pace and rhythm of metropolitan living. "There's nothing about you growing up on a ranch in your bios, both official and unofficial."

"There are some things that don't belong in a bio," he said evenly. "We lived on a ranch from the time I was born until I was fifteen." He leaned back against a stack of hay, his gaze hazy with memories. "I loved it. There's no better way to spend a childhood than on a ranch with lots of animals, hard work and fresh air."

His features tightened, the pleasant smile fading away beneath the strength of a frown. "Unfortunately, my father wasn't very good at ranching. When I was fifteen the bank repossessed the house and the land."

"Oh, how sad." Angela fought the impulse to lean out and touch him, comfort him in some way for the trauma he must have suffered at such a tender age.

He shrugged, as if the loss hadn't bothered him,

although Angela knew differently. "It was probably the best thing that ever happened for my father. We moved in with his brother and he joined my uncle in his dry-cleaning store. They were at the right place at the right time and within a couple of years they had five dry-cleaning shops and more money than they knew what to do with."

Despite his words, Angela sensed a hurt deep inside him, an ache for a home lost, a forced displacement that had been beyond his control. For the first time she had a feeling there was a lot more to her boss than the playboy, driven businessman she'd perceived him as. There was a soft center, a surprising vulnerability that was both evocative and disturbing.

She shoved the disturbing assessment aside. She didn't want to think of Hank as anything but her boss, a man who was paying her handsomely to pretend to be his wife. A man who would never, ever, in reality give her a second glance.

Hank had no idea why he'd told her about losing the family ranch. It was something he'd never told anyone else in his life. It was information that showed up on no bio, a painful episode that had created in him a drive for wealth and success, for the kind of invulnerability money and power bought.

As they walked to the stables, he studied her, as if he might find in her features the reason for his atypical disclosure to her.

Maybe it was because she was so unlike the women he chose to date. Less attractive, less vivacious, Angela lacked the sophisticated veneer of the women he was normally drawn to. Yet, there was something about her that had opened him up. She had a natural warmth that radiated an invitation for confessions.

Curious, he mused. He was rarely one to share much of himself. Surely it had been an anomaly, not likely to happen again.

"You know, on the drive here we talked about our marriage, we talked about our wedding, but we didn't talk about our hobbies." He looked at her curiously. "What do you do in your spare time?"

"Spare time?" She looked at him as if he'd spoken a foreign language.

He grinned ruefully. "Remind me when we get back to the office to cut back on your hours. I've been a slave driver with you for too long."

"I don't mind," she replied, her features radiating solemn earnesty. "I love working for you... when the work is teaching me the advertisement business." They stopped walking as they reached the stable doors. "It's when I'm doing your personal errands that I sort of resent the time spent."

Her cheeks flushed with a hint of pink. "I would rather learn what you know about advertising than be the one to order roses for your latest jilted lover." The color in her cheeks intensified and she

looked away, as if the word "lover" was more than
a little bit naughty.

"Angela, the women I send roses to aren't always my 'lovers,'" he protested. "Sometimes they
are business associates...or friends...or just women
I'm seeing, but not sleeping with."

"Right," she replied dryly, her tone of voice letting him know she didn't believe him.

Suddenly it became important to him that she did
believe him. "You sound like you think I've got
the morals of an alley cat, and that's not true."

She had the most expressive face he'd ever seen.
Emotions flitted across it...disbelief, followed by
uncertainty and at the same time he watched the
fleeting play of her inner feelings he realized her
eyes were brown. Not a plain, ordinary brown, but
a golden amber that radiated warmth that washed
over him like rays of sunshine.

A discordant bell rang in the distance, breaking
the moment of strange captivation that had momentarily seized him. Looking toward the house, he saw
Brody standing on the back porch ringing a large
triangle dinner bell.

"Looks like it's time to eat," he said. "And time
to put our married faces back on."

As they walked back toward the house, Hank
shoved away that momentary need to convince her
of his high moral fiber. He didn't care what she
thought of him. She was his secretary and nothing
more. She did her job efficiently and had agreed to

go along with this crazy game of wife for a week. That's all that mattered to him.

Dinner was a pleasant affair. Angela and Hank were introduced to the other two couples who would share the week of marital enrichment with them. The first couple was Trent and Elena Richards, neighbors of the Robinsons.

"Trent has been my unofficial ranch consultant since we moved here," Brody explained. "He's working with his brother-in-law, and they are quickly becoming known as the place to buy purebred horses."

Trent was a big, handsome man, and his wife Elena was a dark-haired beauty who gazed at Trent as if he'd hung the moon.

Hank found himself wondering why they were here. The way they looked at each other, their constant casual touching, everything about them spoke of their love and commitment for each other. From what they said, they'd been married two years and had a sixteen-month-old little boy.

The other couple, Stan and Edie Watkins, told the group that they had been married ten years. Stan worked as a general manager for the Brody's Biscuits factory in Chicago and Edie worked as a substitute teacher. They had no children and from the look on Edie's face as she told them that, the subject was a painful one.

Hank had spent little time with married people. Most of his time was spent either at work or dating, or alone. For him, it was interesting to watch the other couples, see the easy, comfortable way the husbands and wives interacted with each other.

Still, Hank had always believed marriage involved giving up pieces of yourself that you never got back. He had no pieces he wanted to share with anyone. Marriage might be okay for other people. It just wasn't right for him.

After dinner, the four couples left the table and went into the library for after-dinner drinks. As was customary at social gatherings, it wasn't long before the women had grouped together on one side of the room, and the men on the other.

As Stan asked ranching questions to Trent and Brody, Hank found his attention torn between listening to the men and watching the women.

Angela had surprised him by holding her own in conversation over the meal. She was always so quiet at the office, but not so this evening. She'd shared in a lively political debate, her natural wit bringing laughter to them all several times.

He tried to imagine Sheila in a similar setting, but couldn't. For Sheila, discussing politics meant talking about what outfit the first lady had worn to a particular social function.

"Hank." Brody's large hand fell on his shoulder. "That's a fine woman you married," he said, smiling broadly across the room to Angela. "I always knew you were a smart businessman, but I have to confess, I'd had my doubts about your smarts in your personal life. Seems I was wrong." Brody frowned thoughtfully. "What I don't understand is why in all the interviews I've read about you, she's never mentioned."

"Angela doesn't care much for being in the spotlight. She prefers a low profile," Hank replied.

"She's a bright girl and very personable. You're a lucky man," Brody exclaimed. His face lit with a deeper, fuller smile as he gazed at his own wife. "I know all about being a lucky man." He looked at his male guests. "I'll tell you this. None of you will be the same after this week. You'll be richer spiritually, closer than ever to the women you love after completing my wife's marriage encounter.

"Now, who is ready for another drink?" Brody asked as he removed his hand from Hank's shoulder.

"I'll take a refill," Hank replied. He had a feeling he was going to need it. The guilt of his deception weighed heavily on him. He shoved aside the feeling.

One week. It certainly wasn't like being married for the rest of his life. For one week he could pretend anything. He looked back over at his secretary. Surely for the space of seven days he could pretend he loved her.

"Why don't we all move to the back patio?" Barbara suggested to the entire group. "This time of the evening it is so pleasant outside." She opened double French doors that led out onto a large patio with floral furniture.

As they all moved outside, the segregation by sex

ended. Trent sat at one of the patio tables next to his wife. Stan joined Edie on a love seat and Hank sank down next to Angela on a double glider.

Barbara was right. It was pleasant outside. The heat of the afternoon had passed and a cool light breeze brought with it the fragrance of sweet-smelling flowers and the earthy scent of nearby pastures.

Again the conversation was light and easy... focused on the weather, the approach of winter and ranching life in general. As the talk remained socially shallow and impersonal, Hank felt himself begin to relax. And as he relaxed, he became aware of sensations he hadn't noticed before.

His leg was pressed against Angela's, and he could feel the heat from her body radiating through his jeans. Her clean, fresh-scented perfume seemed to surround him and he noticed that the deepening golden hues of twilight painted her features with a becoming soft glow.

"You doing okay?" he asked in a voice low enough so nobody else could hear.

"Fine," she replied, leaning closer to him. "I amaze myself with my capacity to lie. I never dreamed I'd be so good at it."

"Yeah, I'm going to have to watch you more closely when we get back to the office," he teased.

"Okay, you two whispering lovebirds," Brody said, interrupting their covert conversation. "I'll bet you're all wondering exactly what's going to happen this week. If you think the week is going to be eating good Montana beef and enjoying the quaint little town of Mustang, you're right. But it's going to be a lot more than that.'' Brody threw an arm around his wife's shoulder. ''I figure now is a good time for Barbara to let you know what to expect as far as scheduling is concerned.''

Barbara smiled at them all. ''First, I promise this will be a wonderful, enlightening experience for all of you. Whether you've been married ten years or ten days, this program is designed to deepen your intimacy, connect you and your spouse in a healthy, soulful relationship that will make your marriage better, happier, and completely fulfilling.''

''I think I liked the part about eating Montana beef better,'' Stan said. The others laughed as Edie elbowed him in the ribs.

Barbara laughed with the rest of them. ''I know, it sounds a little scary, but I promise you'll be different people by the end of the week...better husbands and better wives.''

Hank's stomach tightened with anxiety. He didn't want to become a different person. He was satisfied with the man he was at this moment. That's exactly what he didn't like about marriage...women always expected their mates to change.

''We'll start at nine in the morning,'' Barbara continued. ''We'll work from nine until noon as a group. Then after lunch, I'll work with each couple individually for an hour each.'' She smiled at Hank and Angela. ''I'll be starting with you two at one o'clock in the afternoon. After your individual work, you'll be free until dinnertime at six. After dinner, we'll have another group session from eight until nine. And that will be the daily schedule for the rest of the week.'' She looked at them all expectantly. ''Any questions?''

''About a million,'' Stan replied. ''But I guess I'll just wait for the morning to come and they'll all get answered.''

''Anyone else?'' Barbara asked.

Hank wanted to ask if he could back out, if it was too late to get in the car and go back home, back to his office and his familiar life.

Angela laughed aloud. ''Do you notice how we women all look eager and the men all look as if they're ready to bolt?''

The couples looked at each other. It was true. All three men had moved to the edge of their seats, as if ready to take off running at any moment. Everyone laughed, the male laughter holding an edge of discomfort.

Barbara nodded. ''Don't worry, guys, it's perfectly natural. Men are always the most reluctant to change. They are above all, creatures of habit.'' She smiled affectionately at her husband. ''My own, included. But, I think Brody can assure you that as I stated before, this isn't painful and you'll be happier after going through the process.''

Brody nodded. ''I chose the three of you to experience this week because I like you. I consider you all not only business associates, but friends as well. I want you all to have the kind of marriage Barbara and I have. She had to teach me how to give completely of myself, and she's going to teach you the same things."

Barbara stood. "And now I'm going to call it a night. Please feel free to remain out here as long as you want or make yourself at home inside. I'll see you all in the morning."

"Breakfast is at seven-thirty," Brody said as he got up from his chair. "Good night." He followed his wife from the patio.

For a long moment silence followed their parting. The twilight had deepened as night clouds crossed the sky, ready to usurp what little light was left.

"I don't know about the rest of you, but I'm terrified," Stan said, breaking the silence.

Edie giggled. "Honestly Stan, you act like you expect Barbara to perform a lobotomy on you."

"Maybe she will. Maybe that's how she makes us better men," he replied, his words once again causing laughter.

"I suppose if we're going to have such a big day tomorrow, becoming a new man and all, I should turn in," Stan said.

Edie nodded her agreement and smiled apologetically to the others. "We're on eastern time, so our bodies are telling us it's bedtime."

Trent touched his wife's shoulder and they stood as well. "I think we'll head up, too."

Within minutes everyone had left the patio except Hank and Angela. For a moment they sat side by side, the only sound the constant noise of insects clicking and whirring their nighttime lullaby. Far in the distance a cow mooed, the sound somehow lonely and mournful.

"I'm not a bit tired," Angela said, breaking the relative silence. In her voice Hank heard a touch of anxiety.

He had a feeling her unease was born in the knowledge that eventually they would be going up to the same bedroom for the night.

He had no words to say to assuage her uneasiness. She certainly already knew he wouldn't make a pass at her. He knew she wasn't uneasy because of anything he might do. He suspected it was the situation itself she was nervous with, the idea of spending the night in a man's room. An intimate setting that would undoubtably be a novel experience for her.

"No matter how long we put it off, eventually we're going to have to go upstairs to the bedroom," he said softly.

"I know," she said, her tone a touch defensive. "I was just commenting that I wasn't tired."

"You sounded like you might be a little nervous. I realize this might be a bit awkward for you, that perhaps you've never spent the night with a man before."

Despite the falling darkness, he saw the flush that colored her cheeks. But, when she turned to look at him, it wasn't embarrassment that flashed in her eyes. It was anger. "And what makes you think I've never spent the night with a man before? What makes you think I haven't had a lover...or a dozen lovers?'' Her voice was clipped, curt, with a touch of arrogance he found attractive.

''I...uh...just assumed...'' Hank's voice trailed off as he fought with uncomfortable embarrassment.

''You just assumed because I'm not drop-dead gorgeous that I haven't had lovers? You think because I'm not blond and big chested that no man in his right mind would find me desirable?''

''No...that's not it at all,'' Hank interjected hurriedly, surprised at her instantaneous fury. ''It has nothing to do with the way you look.'' He searched for words to explain his thoughts. ''I...you... there's an innocence about you...I just thought probably you were rather inexperienced.''

''It's smarter to ask than to assume,'' she said stiffly.

He hesitated a moment, knowing he shouldn't ask, but unable to stop himself. ''So...how many lovers have you had?''

She eyed him levelly. ''That, Hank Riverton, is none of your business.'' She stood. ''And now, I believe I'll go to bed.'' Without waiting for him, or turning back to look at him, she left the patio.

Hank stared after her. My, he'd certainly managed to ruffle her feathers. And she'd certainly managed to put him in his place, at the same time stirring up more than a little curiosity.

He had a feeling there was a lot more to his secretary than met the eye. He had a feeling it was going to be a week to remember.

Chapter Four

As Angela walked up the staircase to the room where she would be staying for the next week, she wondered if by the time the week was over she would still have a job.

She'd alternated between mouthiness and defensiveness since the moment Hank had picked her up, two traits that were not characteristic of her.

But, there was something about Hank that set her on edge, something that made her more sensitive than normal. Whenever he looked at her, she was aware of her failings...of the fact that she wasn't pretty, she wasn't smooth or sophisticated.

And what on earth was she doing pretending that she took lovers as casually and as often as she took baths?

She shook her head, wondering where in the past

several hours she'd lost her mind. Entering the attractive bedroom, she tried to still the nervous anxiety that winged through her as she thought of sharing the space with Hank for the next six nights.

Opening one of the drawers, she pulled out a pair of pajamas and all the items she needed for a shower. A few minutes later as she stood in the shower, new horrors crossed her mind.

What if she snored? What if in her sleep she ground her teeth or, heaven forbid, drooled? How could she ever face Hank again in a working situation if she did one of those things?

She should have never agreed to this. She lathered her hair with a vengeance, wishing she could go back to that moment when his sinful blue eyes had pleaded with her to agree to this madcap scheme. That's when she'd truly lost her mind, she realized. The moment he'd batted those bedroom eyes at her and she'd agreed to be his pretend wife, she'd skidded out of reality and into temporary insanity.

All too quickly she finished her shower and was clad in the cotton pajamas she'd bought specifically for the trip. Long-sleeved, long-legged, the pale pink pajamas covered her from neck to ankle.

She opened the bathroom door and peeked into the bedroom, grateful to see that Hank had yet to come into the room. Quickly, she took the bedspread off the bed and grabbed the top sheet. If she was going to sleep on the love seat, at least she intended to use a sheet.

She turned off the light overhead and instead turned on the lamp by the bed. With the glow of the softer illumination, she tucked one end of the sheet into the back of the love seat cushions, giving her a section to lie on, then pulled the remainder of the sheet over to cover her.

Angela was no giant. At five foot four inches, she was fairly small. But the love seat wasn't made to be used as a bed, and her legs hung uncomfortably over the wooden, unpadded arm.

Finding this position impossible, she turned on her side and curled her legs up to fit into the small space. If she were lucky, she would be sound asleep by the time Hank came in.

At the moment that thought crossed her mind, the door opened and Hank entered. Angela quickly closed her eyes, feigning sleep.

She could tell what he was doing by the sounds he made. He emptied his pocket on the top of the dresser, the loose change jingling softly as he set it down. She heard him expel a soft sigh at the same time the mattress springs announced that he'd sat on the edge.

Klunk. He removed one shoe.

Klunk. He removed the other.

A drawer opened, then closed, then the bathroom door closed and a moment later she heard the sound of the water running in the shower.

She opened her eyes and shifted positions. Thank goodness. One leg had already fallen asleep. Pins and needles tingled through it as she moved it back and forth to restore the flow of blood.

She shifted again, trying position after position in an effort to get comfortable enough to sleep. She froze again when she heard the sound of the water being shut off.

A few moments later the bathroom door opened and Hank walked back into the room, bringing with him the scent of minty soap and clean male. It was the most provocative scent she'd ever smelled. She wished she had a cold. She wished her nose was stuffed.

She wondered what he slept in. Pajamas? Boxers? Surely he wouldn't sleep nude, not with her in the same room. She squeezed her eyes more tightly closed, refusing to satisfy her curiosity by peeking.

"You can relax, Angela," he said softly. "I'm decent."

She opened her eyes and saw him clad in a pair of red athletic shorts. Decent? She supposed, although the width of his broad chest decorated with dark hair was definitely indecent. As was his flat abdomen, slim hips and long muscular legs.

When she'd had her silly little crush on him, she'd tried to imagine what he'd look like beneath the tailored suits he always wore to the office. Nothing in her fantasies had prepared her for the reality.

He sat on the side of the bed. "Ready for lights out?" he asked.

"Yes." She desperately hoped he didn't notice that her voice was a full octave higher than normal.

She wanted the lights out more than she wanted anything in her life. She didn't want another minute of having to look at him.

She breathed easier as he clicked the switch on the lamp and the room was plunged into darkness.

Within seconds her eyes adjusted and she realized the room wasn't completely dark. There was enough moonlight seeping in through the window to allow her to see Hank as he got into bed and pulled the spread up around him.

"Good night, Angela," Hank said, his voice far too deep, far too intimate for her comfort.

"'Night," she replied, trying to lie still.

He breathed a deep sigh, as if the mattress beneath him was infinitely comfortable. The rat, she thought irritably. She'd probably be crippled by morning. The floor would probably be more comfortable than the damnable love seat.

If she was going to continue the marriage facade for the next week, she needed to get a good night sleep. She had to be on her toes, thinking clearly in order to continue their married pretense. The floor or the love seat, neither would afford her a good night's sleep.

A light snore erupted from Hank. Of course he would fall asleep instantly. He was enjoying the nice softness of a mattress. She looked over at him in irritation. He was on his back, his mouth opened slightly. Even snoring he looked attractive.

What looked more attractive was the half of the bed that was empty. There was plenty of room for her. They were both adults. He certainly wasn't attracted to her and she wasn't sure she even liked him very much. Why couldn't they share the bed?

The two hundred fifty dollars he'd offered her for him getting the bed wasn't enough. It was silly for her to spend a miserable night on the love seat while half the bed remained empty.

Decision made, she stood and grabbed the sheet and wrapped it around her like a cotton cocoon. On tiptoe, not making a sound, she crept to the opposite side of the bed and eased down next to him.

He stirred, turned his head and gave her a sleepy grin. "You're forfeiting part of your bonus."

"It's worth it," she replied as her body conformed to the soft mattress. "That love seat is a torture device."

He laughed, a deep soft rumble that echoed in the pit of her stomach. "Good night." Almost immediately he was back asleep.

It took Angela longer to fully relax. Although there was a full six inches between their bodies, she could feel Hank's warmth. His clean, freshly showered scent surrounded her.

She closed her eyes and concentrated on lying still, breathing deep and fully. Within minutes she was asleep.

Something tickled her nose. Brian with a feather duster, she thought. Her brother was such a tease. He was always pulling some prank or another.

She frowned, something not quite right. Mustang,

Montana. She was in Mustang, Montana. What was Brian doing here?

As the last vestige of sleep fell away, Angela opened her eyes. Skin. That's the first thing she saw. Tanned skin with dark hair...hair that tickled her nose.

Hank's chest. What on earth was she doing with her face on Hank's chest? She didn't move, was afraid to. His breathing was deep and regular and she assumed he was still asleep.

One of his arms was around her, his hand resting lightly at the small of her back. Their legs were tangled together, how and when they had become that way, Angela had no clue.

Still, for a long moment she did nothing but remain unmoving, finding pleasure in the easy way their bodies had found each other in sleep. She could feel his heartbeat beneath her cheek, a faint rhythm that seemed provocatively intimate.

The first rays of morning peeked in through the curtains, golden shards of light that lit the room in a surreal illumination. Surreal. The entire experience of being in Hank's arms felt surreal.

"Good morning." His chest vibrated as he spoke.

Angela shot up and away from him, nearly falling off the side of the bed as she tugged her legs away from his. "I thought you were still asleep," she exclaimed.

"I've been awake for a while, but you seemed

to be sleeping so soundly, I didn't want to bother you.''

''I was. I was sound asleep…completely unconscious asleep.'' She wanted him to know that she hadn't willfully, consciously draped herself across him. How embarrassing. How utterly mortifying.

He grinned and stretched with arms overhead, looking like a majestic lion awakening from a nap. ''I slept great. What about you?''

She nodded, wanting to get up and out of the bed, yet subtly captivated by the notion of being in bed with him. She was definitely crazy, she decided. But, what a pleasant delusion. ''I slept well once I decided to forego the love seat.''

He rolled over on his side and braced his elbow beneath him. His eyes were the deep blue of fathomless water, his jaw darkened with a morning shadow of whiskers. His hair was disheveled, strands skewed this way and that, and yet Angela had never seem him look more handsome, more masculine.

She remained sitting up, knowing her hair was a mess and not a stitch of makeup adorned her face. No mascara to darken her pale lashes, no lipstick to add color to her lips. Nothing to hide behind.

She flushed beneath the intensity of his gaze. ''You're staring at me,'' she said with an uneasy laugh.

''Yes, I am,'' he agreed. He reached out and touched a strand of her long, curly hair. ''Why do you tie it back all the time?''

"It's too curly and wild."

"It's beautiful." He dropped his hand and sat up, a slight, irritated look crossing his face. He picked up his watch from the nightstand. "We'd better get dressed and ready for breakfast. It's already almost seven."

"You can use the bathroom first," she offered.

"Fine." Without hesitation, he got out of the bed, grabbed clothes for the day and disappeared into the bathroom.

Angela stared at the closed door, wondering what had irritated him. Her hair? That didn't even make sense. He'd said her hair was beautiful. Warmth suffused her as she remembered those words.

Perhaps seeing her without makeup, her features completely unadorned, had scared him up and out. Maybe he was irritated over the fact that she'd half smothered him while sleeping. God, how embarrassing. And it was only the first night.

She still had five nights left to sleep with Hank. She shivered at the thought, disturbed by the fact she wasn't sure if the shiver was brought on by fear...or delight.

The morning session whizzed by without any problems. Hank mentally worked on a new ad campaign for one of his accounts while Barbara lectured them on the history of marriage and the reasons why the institution was so important to society. Hank cared about neither.

Angela sat next to him, appearing to listen intently to Barbara's every word. He cast Angela a surreptitious gaze. As usual, her hair was tied back in an untidy knot at the nape of her neck. The dark brown curls absolutely refused to be confined, springing free from the barrette that attempted to maintain order.

It had been odd, waking up with her asleep nearly on top of him. Her soft breathing had caressed his chest and he'd felt the press of her breasts against his side. Initially, when he'd awakened, his first impulse had been to spring up, disentangle from her as quickly as possible before she woke up. But, the longer he'd waited to move, the more pleasant the sensations that whispered through him.

Her body had fit so perfectly against his. She'd felt both small and vulnerable in sleep, yet sexy and alluring at the same time.

When he'd touched her hair, felt the silky softness of a curly strand, warmth had shot through him, a warmth far too appealing. The physical desire that had speared through him had both shocked and surprised him.

He valued Angela's secretarial and management skills far too much to risk losing them by having sex with her. And that's what it would be…having sex, not making love. He had a feeling that Angela would want more…she would want lovemaking, not just sex for desire's sake. And even though he knew it was none of his business, he still wondered just how many lovers she'd had in the past.

"We'll break for lunch now," Barbara said,

drawing Hank's attention away from the woman
next to him. "We'll be serving in about fifteen
minutes," she explained.

Lunch passed far too quickly and all too soon it
was time for Hank and Angela to join Barbara in
the library for their "personal" marriage workshop.

"I'd like for the two of you to sit on the floor
and face each other," Barbara said as she closed
the library door, giving the three of them complete
privacy. She gestured to a plush, thick throw rug in
front of the fireplace.

Hank sank down as Angela did the same. He
wondered if his facial features held the same anxiety that Angela's expressed. As they faced each
other, he saw the tension that thinned her lips and
darkened her eyes. He had a feeling this would be
the first real test of their "marriage" and he knew
Angela realized the same thing.

Could they pull it off? Could they make Barbara
believe that they'd been married for two years,
shared intimate secrets with each other, worked together toward common goals and dreams?

"Come on, get closer together. Make your knees
touch," Barbara instructed. They moved closer,
their knees meeting each other's. Barbara sat down
on a chair some distance from them.

"Often in the courtship game and an ensuing
marriage," she began, "the two people involved
don't share everything with each other. There are
pieces of their past, events from their childhood that

made them who they are, and it's often these milestones we don't share but rather guard inside.''

She smiled at Hank and Angela. ''Today you're going to share those places with each other. Now, I want you to hold hands.''

Hank took Angela's hands in his, surprised by how soft, how utterly feminine they were. He'd never noticed before, but she had pretty hands, with long slender fingers and neatly shaped nails painted a pearly pink. The nail polish astounded him and oddly touched him, so utterly female in his no-nonsense, efficient secretary.

She squeezed his hands and he didn't know if she was attempting to assure him or communicating to him she needed assurance. He squeezed back, wondering if she had any idea how nervous he was.

It was crazy. He wheeled and dealed with millions of dollars at stake and never broke into a sweat. But this little exercise of Barbara's had him more nervous than he'd ever been in his life.

''Okay, we'll start with Angela. Angela, I want you to share with Hank the very best day you can remember from the time you were small until you were eighteen years old.''

''That's easy,'' Angela replied, her gaze still on Barbara. ''The day my mother brought my baby brother home from the hospital.''

''Don't tell me,'' Barbara exclaimed. She pointed to Hank. ''Tell him. Tell him everything about the day and how you felt at that time.''

Angela directed her gaze to Hank. ''I was nine

years old when Brian was born. By then my father was gone and my mother was sick a lot, so I knew I was going to play a big role in the everyday raising of Brian.''

She smiled, a smile that lit her eyes and caused golden warmth to flow from them. ''He looked more like a monkey than a baby. He had a head full of dark hair and his face was wrinkled up like an old man's.'' She laughed at the memory, and the sound of her pleasant laughter shot through Hank like a warm swallow of good liquor.

''But the minute his little fingers closed around my thumb, I knew I'd do anything for him,'' she continued. ''I knew the first moment I saw him that he was going to be a big responsibility, and a lot of that responsibility would be on my shoulders. But, I didn't care. It was a labor of love.''

Hank remembered that moment when he'd stepped into her house and saw her wrestling with her brother. Her cheeks had been flushed with her exertion, but her eyes, her features, all had been lit with the love she had for her brother.

That same smile lit her face now, transforming her from average to almost beautiful. ''I knew on that day, I was no longer Angela Samuels, daughter of Roger and Janette Samuels. On that day, I was Angela Samuels, big sister to Brian Samuels.''

Her smile fell away and her expression grew thoughtful. ''I knew even then that as long as I loved him, that little baby boy would love me unconditionally. It was the absolute best day of my life.''

"And your brother still loves you unconditionally,'' Hank replied softly, remembering the love that had so obviously flowed between brother and sister the morning he'd come to Angela's house to pick her up.

Angela smiled. "Most of the time. Now, it's your turn. The happiest day in your life was when?''

Hank frowned thoughtfully, trying to remember a day in his life that could equal what she'd just shared with him. "The day I got my first horse.'' The words fell from his lips unbidden, a picture-memory filled his head. He smiled as the memory unfurled in his mind. It had been years since he'd thought of that day.

"I was seven at the time,'' he said. "I came home from school and my dad told me to go out to the barn and get him some rope. I went out to the barn and started to grab a length of rope and that's when I heard the deep snorting of an animal, the stomping of horse hooves.''

For a moment Hank was back in that old, dilapidated barn. At seven years old, what he wanted more than anything else in the world was a horse of his own. He'd considered himself a cowboy, but it was impossible to be a cowboy without a horse.

"We didn't have any horses. Still, I followed the sound to the last stable, and there she was…the prettiest young mare in the world. She looked at me with her liquid brown eyes, nuzzled my chest as if searching for my heart, and I knew then that we were going to be best buddies for a long time to come.''

''What did you name her?''

''Bandit. She had a dark mask around her eyes and it was easy to see that was what her name should be.'' Hank sighed, the happy memory embracing him. ''I think I knew even then that we were struggling financially, and that only made Dad buying Bandit for me that much more special.''

Angela's features reflected his pleasant memories. Her eyes radiated warmth and her lips were curved upward in a sweet smile of shared reflections from a distant past.

''Good. You two are doing terrific.'' Barbara's voice surprised Hank. For a few moments he had forgotten her presence in the room. ''I can tell by the look on your faces that you're enjoying not only your own memories, but each other's as well. Now I want you do to something a little more difficult. I want you to share with each other the most painful day in your life as you were growing up.''

Hank's first impulse was to jerk his hands from Angela's and say no way. Already he felt as if a small invasion had occurred, an unwelcomed entry into those private places he guarded so well.

It had been years since he'd thought of Bandit, of those carefree days on the ranch where he'd been truly, completely happy. His memories were his own, and he was reluctant to share any of them with anyone.

But, before he could voice any true protest to furthering the exercise, Angela drew a deep breath. "That's an easy one, too. The day my father left," she said. Her expressive features radiated myriad emotions, the strongest one a sadness, a sense of loss so profound, he felt it echo in the deepest chamber of his heart.

He squeezed her hands more tightly as she caught her bottom lip between her teeth, apparently fighting a wave of tears that appeared poised in her eyes, ready to spill onto her cheeks. How quickly the tears had appeared, letting him know the depth of pain left by her father's abandonment.

"I didn't even know he and my mother were having problems. They never fought, Mom was pregnant and I thought everything was fine, my whole world was secure. Then one summer morning I woke up to find Dad packing his clothes."

A single tear fell onto her cheek, and Hank checked the impulse to lean forward and swipe it away.

"He told me he had to leave, that he wasn't happy living with us." She started to speak more, but instead closed her mouth as if to say anything more was too painful.

In the last two days he'd seen her embarrassed, indignant and irritated. In the time of her employment, he'd seen her as efficient, productive and capable. Nothing had prepared him for this soft vulnerability, the painful ache her hurt created inside him. How was it possible that her pain could feel so bad inside him?

"I never saw him again, never heard from him again after that day. He left and never looked back and...and I always wondered if I'd been smarter, better, prettier, would he have stayed?"

Her question hung in the air, containing all the wistful fantasies, all the yearning and sadness of a child abandoned.

"Hank, tell Angela how you feel," Barbara said softly. "Tell her how you feel about what she's shared."

Hank looked into Angela's eyes, saw her need for comfort and realized he couldn't block her pain from his heart. "I feel bad for her. My heart aches with her pain. I wish she'd never had to go through that."

"Tell her," Barbara instructed. "Don't tell me."

"I feel bad for you," he amended. "I...I wish I would have been there, that I had known you then, so I could have told you that it was his loss. He was the one who missed out on knowing what a wonderful person you are, what a loving heart you have."

And she did. Even without knowing her well, Hank knew instinctively that her capacity to love would be awesome. He'd seen it when she'd spoken of her brother.

He wondered what it would be like to be the person on the receiving end of such vast love. Surely it would be beyond spectacular.

"What about you, Hank?" Barbara asked. "Share with Angela the worst day of your life."

Hank frowned thoughtfully for a long moment, then shrugged. "I'm afraid I'm one of those people whose childhood was pretty unremarkable."

"What about your mother's death?" Angela asked.

Hank frowned once again. "I know it sounds terrible, but I was only five at the time. I don't have many memories of the day she died. She'd been hospitalized so much in my early childhood, she was little more than a stranger to me at the time of her death."

He looked at Angela, then back to Barbara. "I'm afraid I just don't have the kind of traumatic memories you're asking me to share."

"What about the sale of the ranch?" Angela asked, instantly making Hank regret telling her that particular information.

"Okay, you're right." He drew an audible breath. "That was a tough day," he agreed.

"Go deeper, Hank," Barbara said. "Let Angela know how you felt that day, your disappointment...your sorrow."

Lie, an inner voice commanded Hank. Make something up to satisfy Barbara, pretend that you're sharing while keeping your thoughts and emotions to yourself. And yet even while he was formulating this plan, the truth spilled out of him.

"The bank didn't just repossess everything. It held an auction, and that day was the blackest of my life." Along with his words came the black despair of that day.

He and his father had stood side by side and watched as farm equipment, furniture, livestock, all the pieces that had been their lives were bid on and sold away for a fraction of their worth.

As if it were happening at this moment in time, the same impotent anger, the same aching grief pierced through him. "Even Bandit was auctioned away." His voice was thick with emotion as he remembered seeing his beloved horse, his constant companion being led to an awaiting trailer.

He'd only felt that aching grief one other time in his life, when he'd been twenty and Sarah Washington had told him she didn't love him anymore.

"Oh Hank. How awful," Angela said, her voice filled with empathy. She leaned toward him, as if willing him to take her in his arms, as if they could find solace in each other's embrace.

"Go on," Barbara urged. "Hold each other. For the next few minutes I want you to hold each other, comfort one another's pain."

Before Hank realized how it happened, Angela was on his lap, her arms wrapped around his neck, her face buried in the hollow of his neck.

Hank closed his eyes and responded, his arms wrapping around her. Her breasts snuggled against his chest, her hips against his as her legs straddled him. It was a provocative position and Hank tried to distance himself from her. But it was impossible.

Her hair smelled of fresh-cut flowers and her

body offered him the warmth of the sun. Barbara's presence was forgotten, the game they played was also forgotten. He refused to think, instead focused only on the pleasure of holding her in his arms.

She raised her head and looked at him. "I'm sorry you lost Bandit," she said, her voice resonant with sweet sincerity. "There's nothing worse than the loss of something you love, something you cherish."

Unable to ignore his impulse, he reached up and touched a strand of hair that had managed to work itself loose from the barrette at the nape of her neck. "And I'm sorry your father was a stupid fool," he replied. "And he was, you know...to leave you behind."

"I'd like you two to continue to comfort each other for another ten minutes, then the exercise is officially over." Barbara walked to the door and smiled at them. "I'll see you this evening at dinner." She left the library.

The moment the door closed behind Barbara, Hank knew he should release Angela. The game was over for the moment. Without Barbara's presence there was no need to pretend anymore.

But at the moment, letting go of Angela seemed impossible. He wanted her warmth against him. He wanted her arms around him. He wanted them to continue to comfort each other as the wounds they'd opened slowly eased, mended as best they could.

As Hank gazed at the woman he held in his arms,

he realized he didn't intend to release her until he did one more thing. It was stupid, it was crazy, but he wouldn't be deterred by anything as ridiculous as good sense.

He drew in a breath, then captured her lips with his own.

Chapter Five

Amazing...how lips that appeared thin and unwelcoming could in reality be so soft, taste so good. Initially, the kiss lingered softly...a tentative touch of lips against lips. However, it wasn't long before that wasn't enough.

Hank touched his tongue to hers. Desire roared through him like a flash fire as she opened her mouth, allowing him to deepen the kiss.

She tasted of innocence and simmering sensuality, an intoxicating combination that shot straight to his head. He drank of her, loving her taste.

He felt a thundering heartbeat, but didn't know if it was hers or his own. Rubbing his hands up her back, he felt how delicate she was and a fierce uncharacteristic protectiveness rose up inside him.

She arched her back beneath his caress, like a cat

enjoying and encouraging the warmth of a stroking hand. As she arched, her breasts pressed against his chest, as if taunting him to touch, to explore their fullness beneath the cotton material that covered them. He hesitated, afraid of his need, afraid he'd frighten her away.

Then he knew the heartbeat was his own, loudly pounding the rhythm of want, of need. He was vaguely aware of the sound of their breathing, short and sharp as their tongues warred and their mouths remained locked together.

He reached up behind her, grasped the barrette that held her hair and fumbled with it until the clasp released and her thick curls spilled into his hands.

The moment her hair was freed, she pulled her mouth from his and stumbled to her feet. "Why... why did you do that?" she asked, her voice weak and breathless.

She bent and picked up the barrette from where it had fallen to the floor. He noticed that her hands trembled and her cheeks were stained a vivid pink.

"Do what?" he asked inanely, trying to gain time to get himself under control, to get the sweet taste of her out of his mouth. He was stunned by his reaction to the kiss, dazed by the depths of his desire.

"Kiss me. Why did you kiss me?" She didn't look at him, but instead stared just past him as her hands worked to gather her hair and refasten the barrette.

He shrugged. "If you didn't like it, then why did you kiss me back?"

Her cheeks flushed deeper in hue and he noticed that her hands still shook as she finished with her hair. "I didn't say that I didn't like it. I just asked why you did it."

Hank stood and raked a hand through his hair. "I don't know," he admitted truthfully. "It just seemed like the thing to do at the time. I'm sorry. I was way out of line." It was the first time in his life he could ever remember feeling the need to apologize for a kiss.

"It's all right," she conceded, her gaze finally meeting his. She smiled tightly. "You just took me by surprise. You didn't mention kissing as part of my job description."

He drew a deep breath, needing his heartbeat to slow, his breathing to return to a more normal pace. "Don't worry, I promise it won't be a part of your normal, usual job."

He raked a hand through his hair, still unsteady. "Look, we've got a couple of hours before dinner. Why don't we take a drive into Mustang, check out the local color?" Maybe a couple hours away from this ranch, away from Brody and Barbara would put things back in their perspective.

At the moment Hank felt slightly off-kilter, a little woozy around the edges. The confession time with Angela, followed by the surprisingly sexy kiss had momentarily disoriented him.

For just a moment he'd forgotten that the woman

he held, the woman he kissed was his secretary, mousy little Angela.

For just a moment, as he'd held her in his arms, her features had lit with an inner glow that had made her appear distractingly attractive.

He didn't want to think of her as pretty, and he damned straight didn't want to think of her as a sexy woman, or one he desired.

He needed her as his secretary. He couldn't afford to complicate things with her and wind up losing her in all capacities.

"Maybe we could get a cup of coffee, kick around some ideas for the Martindale account." It was a shameless ploy to get things back on track between them.

"Really?" She eyed him dubiously. "You'll let me help on the Martindale account?"

"Sure." He opened the library door, feeling as if he needed fresh air to clear his head.

"Okay. Just let me grab my purse from the room." While Angela ran to the room for her purse, Hank stepped out on the front veranda to wait for her.

He wasn't sure what it was about the kiss he'd shared with her that bothered him so much. It hadn't been a long kiss, at least not by his usual standard.

Still, electrical pulses had leaped through his veins as his mouth had covered hers. His breathing had quickened and his body had responded instantaneously, as if preparing him for a bout of passionate lovemaking.

He drew in a deep breath, adrenaline surging as if he'd just faced a life or death kind of crisis. It had been crazy. A momentary flirt with insanity. He'd definitely have to be more careful for the remainder of the week. Somehow the exercise Barbara had them do had made him vulnerable... needy.

Angela's comfort, her intimate nearness, had touched his heart in areas he'd never bared before. Her sweet embrace had made him want more of her and for a moment he'd lost touch with reality and instead had plunged into the fantasy he and Angela had created. For a single, solitary moment, he'd almost felt as if he were married to her.

He saw Brody in the distance, talking on a cellular phone while he oiled a harness. Brody waved, and Hank waved back, wishing he hadn't gotten himself into this mess. He should have just told Brody the truth, but instead he'd come up with a plan that suddenly didn't seem like such a good idea.

He walked out to where Brody was working and told him that he and Angela were taking a ride into town.

As he walked back to the porch, Hank again reminded himself that he definitely had to be more careful. The last thing he wanted was for the lines between reality and fantasy to somehow become blurred.

* * *

Angela grabbed her purse from the dresser, then paused to stare at her reflection in the mirror. Her cheeks were pink and her lips looked red and swollen. She touched her lips, remembering Hank's kiss. Warmth flooded through her as she remembered those moments when his lips had claimed hers.

It had been her first, true adult kiss, and the power of it had stolen not only her breath, but her sense as well. She'd been mindless beneath his mastery, stunned with the desire that soared through her.

If he'd wanted, he could have had her right there, in the middle of the library floor. He could have made love to her and she would have done nothing to stop him, rather she would have actively encouraged him.

Her cheeks flamed with renewed warmth and she turned away from the mirror. It was Barbara's fault. The crazy exercise of talking about good and bad times, of sharing happy and painful moments, had done exactly what it was supposed to do…created a bond, an intimacy that would enrich the relationship of the two people involved.

But, she and Hank weren't involved, and there was no relationship, other than boss and secretary. She couldn't forget that.

So, why had he kissed her? Barbara hadn't been in the room, there had been no need to carry the pretense of their marriage any further. He'd said it just seemed like the thing to do. She knew the smartest thing she could do at the moment was forget the kiss ever took place.

A few minutes later she met him on the porch, emotions firmly in check. "Ready," she announced.

"I saw Brody just a moment ago," he said as they walked to the grassy area near the detached garage where his car was parked. "I told him we wouldn't be back for dinner, that we would get something to eat in town."

She looked at him in surprise. "Okay," she agreed.

"I did tell him we'd be back in time for the evening session." Hank opened the passenger car door for her.

She slid into the car, wondering what had made him decide that they would eat in town. Maybe he felt the need to be with other people...people besides the ones they were trying to fool.

She felt the same kind of need, the desire to distance herself from him, to remember that she was his secretary and nothing more. She'd be a fool to entertain any other thoughts to the contrary. She couldn't forget that she wasn't the type of woman Hank dated.

"It's a beautiful day," she said as Hank turned out of Brody's driveway and onto the road that would take them into Mustang.

"Gorgeous," he agreed. "Although it won't be long and winter will be here. I sure wouldn't want to live out here when the snow starts to fly."

"Why not?" she asked as she looked out across the wide expanse of pasture that surrounded them.

"The winters are hard here, below freezing temperatures, heavy snowfalls. I'm sure a lot of times these people are prisoners in their homes, held captive by the elements."

"I don't know, I think the idea of being snowbound sounds pretty romantic." Angela could imagine a roaring fire in a stone fireplace warming the interior of a little farmhouse while outside a blanket of snow and ice covered the earth. It was easy to envision making love beneath a cozy patchwork quilt in front of the fire.

"How like a woman," Hank replied dryly, "to like the idea of trapping a man into spending quality time with her by praying for a blizzard."

It was the kind of chauvinistic, sexist remark that always raised the hackles on Angela's back. She was almost grateful to him for reminding her that there was a small part of Hank Riverton she didn't like very much.

"I imagine that particular fantasy isn't exclusive to females," she returned evenly. "I'm sure there are plenty of males who fantasize being snowbound with some big-breasted blond bimbo who will fulfill their every need."

"You're right," he conceded with a grin. "I suppose I can see certain advantages to being snowbound for a day or two with somebody like that."

"Yeah, as long as all your needs are in the lower half of your body, you'd be fine," Angela retorted.

Hank laughed, a deep rumble of pleasure. "I can't get over you. At the office you never showed this impudent side. I had no idea you had such a good sense of humor, such a quick mind."

Warm pleasure overtook her at his words. For the past two years that she'd worked for him, she'd known how invisible she was to him.

Surely after this week when they returned to their regular schedule, their relationship as boss and secretary would be subtly changed for the better. Maybe she wouldn't have to seek another job after all. Perhaps this little shared ruse was a blessing in disguise.

For a few minutes they were silent. It was a comfortable silence. Angela enjoyed the pastoral scenery, felt her body relaxing as a direct result of the peaceful surrounding.

Hank slowed his speed as they reached the edge of town. "Brody said the diner on Main is a good place to eat," he said as he turned down Main Street. "He said they have the best pie in the entire state."

"I'll bet it won't be long before he has the diner owner talked into serving Robinson's biscuits for breakfast."

Hank grinned. "It's already a done deal. He gave them a month's free supply of biscuits in order to induce them to try them. Then, when they were renovating the house, he paid the workers extra every morning to go to the diner, order the biscuits and rave about them."

Angela laughed. "Brody is one slick business-man."

Hank pulled the car into a parking space in front of the Mustang Diner. He turned off the engine, then turned to look at Angela. "Angela...about that kiss..." he began, his features radiating awkwardness.

"Stop right there." She held up a hand to him. She knew he felt the need to tell her the kiss didn't mean anything and it irritated her that he thought his kiss so potent that it might make her think he actually cared about her.

"Honestly Hank, you don't have to worry about it. On a scale of one to ten, it wasn't much more than a six. Besides, you aren't my type at all." Before he could reply, she opened the door and got out of the car.

He said nothing to her as they walked to the back of the diner and slid into a booth. She opened a menu and gazed at the selections, but felt his gaze focused solely on her. She looked at him. "What?" she asked.

"A six? You thought it was no more than a six?" He looked at her incredulously.

Angela bit back a burst of laughter, realizing she'd shot an arrow and deflated his ego. "It can't be any more than a six without real emotion behind it."

"Who told you that?"

"It's my scale. I make the rules."

"Your scale stinks," he replied as he slapped

open a menu. "It was at least a nine no matter how you cut it. And what do you mean, I'm not your type?"

"Don't take it personally," Angela said. "I just want more than I think you offer the women you get involved with."

"More? More what?" Hank's features were schooled in frustration, as if he found it unbelievable that he wouldn't be what she wanted in a man.

"More of yourself." Angela closed her menu, sorry she'd gotten herself in the middle of this entire conversation. "I could tell you were uncomfortable with the exercise we did this afternoon. You aren't used to sharing yourself. The man I fall in love with will want to share every piece of himself with me. And he'll want to know everything there is to know about me as well."

Hank frowned. "You give away your power when you share too much of yourself."

"But love shouldn't be about power," Angela protested. "You're approaching love with the same rules you approach business and it's not the same."

They stopped the conversation as the waitress appeared at their booth. They both ordered the daily special and when the waitress left, Angela once again picked up the conversation where they'd left off.

"Love isn't supposed to be a struggle for power, or about learning weaknesses that can be exploited."

He leaned back in the booth and eyed her in

speculation. "If you have all the answers about love, then why are you still single?"

"I don't have all the answers," she protested. "I just know what I want and what I don't want. And I'm still single because I haven't had much time to find Mr. Right. Helping raise Brian and then working for you has left me little time. I just haven't found the man who is right for me yet." She paused a moment, her gaze curious. "What about you? You ever been in love?"

She could tell her question caught him by surprise. He sat forward, took a drink from his water glass, then rubbed a hand across his brow as if fighting a headache. "Once. When I was young and stupid." He rubbed his brow once again, then took another sip of his water.

"What was her name?" Angela asked.

"Sarah. Sarah Washington." An irritated frown stole across his features. "What is this? Twenty Questions? Truth or Dare?"

Angela smoothed her napkin across her lap. "I'm sorry if I touched a nerve."

Hank drew a deep breath. "It's all right," he said grudgingly. He took a drink of his water, then continued, "It was a long time ago. I thought she was my girl, the one who was going to spend the rest of her life with me. I was wrong."

He stared at Angela for a long moment, then shook his head, as if to dismiss whatever thought had crossed his mind. "You have told me a few times you want to be a more active part of the agency. Why don't you tell me any ideas that have crossed your mind concerning the Martindale account?''

Angela knew it was time to change the subject, although she found herself most curious about the young woman who'd once captured Hank's heart only to throw it away.

Through the duration of the meal, they talked about not only the Martindale account, but other accounts as well. Angela shared with him various ideas she'd had to promote companies and encourage sales.

Patiently he explained to her why some of her ideas wouldn't work, and praised her for the ones that showed possibilities. She warmed beneath his tutelage, soaking up what he had to teach her and pleased when she managed to teach him something.

This was the kind of relationship she'd dreamed of when she'd first taken the job as his secretary. She'd wanted to learn, yearned to be taken seriously, wanted a give-and-take that would eventually prove to him how valuable she could be not as his secretary, but as an active participant in the ad business.

They lingered over pie and coffee, sharing a lively debate over everything from politics to the best kind of movies. All too quickly it was time for them to return to Brody's ranch for the evening session.

"You're bright, Angela," Hank said as they drove back toward the ranch. He cast her a look that warmed her from her toes up. "And you're right, I've been wasting your talent having you run my errands. When we get back to the office, there's going to be some changes made."

"I'd like that," she agreed. She leaned back against the seat and smiled happily. If nothing else came out of this crazy week, it was enough that he'd finally realized her potential. It was what she'd wanted ever since she'd started working for him.

Excitement winged through her as she thought of what her job would hopefully entail when they returned. Instead of spending her days making appointments for dinner or ordering flowers, she'd actually get a chance to use her intelligence.

"You have a sharp brain, funny face," her father had said the day before he'd left them forever. "You need to use that brain. Your intelligence will take you far." His eyes had gazed at her with a touch of sadness. "And unfortunately you aren't going to be one of those lucky girls who are going to be able to depend on your good looks."

Angela closed her eyes and tried to shove the painful memory aside. Funny face. That's what he'd always called her. She'd loved her father with all her heart, and for years after he'd left, she'd wondered if she'd been prettier would he have stayed?

She knew better now. She knew that she could have looked like Miss America and he would have left no matter what. It had taken her years to realize that his leaving hadn't been about her...it had been about him.

Later that evening, the three couples sat with Brody and Barbara in the library. Barbara wrapped up the day's activities, what they had learned, what they had yet to explore.

After Barbara finished, the conversation turned to children. Trent and Elena spoke of their little boy, their eyes shining with obvious adoration.

"Travis is a handful," Elena said, "but he's bright and healthy and a daily reminder of our love." Her eyes glowed as she reached for her husband's hand.

Angela yearned for that same sort of connection with a man, and if she were lucky, someday there would be children. Her heart expanded as she thought of a baby, a living, breathing symbol of her love for the special man she hoped one day would share her life.

"Kids," Brody agreed in his loud, blustery voice. "Nothing better in the world than kids. Barbara and I have two, one of each. Of course, they're both grown and with families of their own now, but they're an additional joy to the heart that nobody should do without."

"Unfortunately, Stan and I can't have children," Edie said, the shadows in her eyes letting the others know the depth of her pain on this particular subject. "We've been to all sorts of specialists over the years, but with no luck."

"Last year we decided to adopt and the agency

tells us we should have a little boy or girl very soon now,'' Stan replied. He smiled at his wife and the shadows in her eyes transformed into gleams of pleasure.

''That's right. In fact, they called us last week and said that within the next month there should be a child available for us.''

Edie laughed. ''After ten years of waiting, our spare room is finally going to be used as a nursery.''

There were congratulations all around, then Brody turned his gaze on Hank. ''What about you? Don't tell me you're sacrificing having children for the almighty dollar and the need to get ahead.'' There was something slightly accusatory, subtly condemning in Brody's voice.

''Not at all,'' Hank replied. ''In fact,'' he reached for Angela's hand. ''We weren't going to announce it for a while yet.'' He smiled proudly as a sick dread rolled around in Angela's tummy, definitely a different feeling than the miraculous stir of life within. ''Angela is three-months pregnant.''

Chapter Six

"Are you crazy?" Angela glared at Hank from across the expanse of their bedroom. "Have you utterly lost your mind?"

Hank held his hands out in an effort to placate her, even though he knew he deserved her anger. "I'm sorry. I really don't know what got into me."

But he did know what had made him make the ridiculous declaration. He'd watched the other couples throughout the evening session.

For the first time in his life he'd felt envy. He'd envied them their obvious affection, the bonds that didn't seem to diminish them individually, but rather strengthened them. He'd seen the shine in their eyes as they'd talked of creating families, and he'd wanted that for himself.

"I got caught up in the moment," he finally said.

"Yeah, well while you were getting caught up in the moment you got me pregnant," Angela retorted.

"But, I didn't mean to get you pregnant," Hank replied. The humor in the situation and their words suddenly struck him. He sank down on the edge of the bed and watched as she paced back and forth. "Even though we didn't exactly plan the pregnancy, I promise I'll be right beside you every step of the way, both financially and emotionally."

She stopped her pacing, looked at him sharply, then shook her head with a small laugh, as if she, too, suddenly realized how ridiculous their conversation had become.

She walked over and sat down next to him on the bed. "And what are you going to do in six months when Brody expects to see our child? Dial Rent-A-Baby?"

"Is there such a place?" He laughed at her renewed look of outrage. "I don't know...I can't think ahead that far. I just need to get through this week."

"I should pack my suitcase and go back home, refuse to participate in this charade any further."

He nodded. "And I wouldn't blame you." He raked a hand through his hair and gazed at her. As always, her hair was confined at the nape of her neck and his fingers itched to release it, allow those curls to bounce and dance in his hands.

As he remembered the kiss they had shared, he

GET A FREE TEDDY BEAR...

You'll love this plush, cuddly Teddy Bear, an adorable accessory for your dressing table, bookcase or desk. Measuring 5 ½" tall, he's soft and brown and has a bright red ribbon around his neck – he's completely captivating! And he's yours *absolutely free*, when you accept this no-risk offer!

▶ CLAIM YOUR FREE BOOKS AND FREE GIFT! RETURN THIS CARD TODAY! ▶

AND TWO FREE BOOKS!

Here's a chance to get **two free Silhouette Romance® novels** from the Silhouette Reader Service™ **absolutely free!**

There's no catch. You're under no obligation to buy anything. We charge nothing – ZERO – for your first shipment. And you don't have to make any minimum number of purchases – not even one!

Find out for yourself why thousands of readers enjoy receiving books by mail from the Silhouette Reader Service™. They like the **convenience of home delivery**…they like getting the best new novels months before they're available in bookstores…and they love our **discount prices!**

Try us and see! Return this card promptly. We'll send your free books and a free Teddy Bear, under the terms explained on the back. We hope you'll want to remain with the reader service – but the choice is always yours!

315 SDL CTKP

215 SDL CTKJ
(S-R-10/99)

Name: _____
(PLEASE PRINT)

Address: _____ Apt.#: _____

City: _____ State/Prov.: _____ Postal Zip/Code: _____

NO OBLIGATION TO BUY!

The Silhouette Reader Service™ — Here's how it works:

If offer card is missing write to: Silhouette Reader Service, 3010 Walden Ave., P.O. Box 1867, Buffalo, NY 14240-1867

BUSINESS REPLY MAIL

FIRST-CLASS MAIL   PERMIT NO. 717   BUFFALO, NY

POSTAGE WILL BE PAID BY ADDRESSEE

SILHOUETTE READER SERVICE
3010 WALDEN AVE
PO BOX 1867
BUFFALO NY 14240-9952

NO POSTAGE
NECESSARY
IF MAILED
IN THE
UNITED STATES

felt the desire to taste her lips again, feel her body heat against his own.

It seemed odd to him that he'd ever thought of her as unattractive. Although not classically pretty, she was exotically striking. Her face held a warm glow that made you forget that her features were rather irregular. Her eyes caught and held attention, beautiful pools of golden brown.

"So, have we picked out names for our bundle of joy yet?" she asked, pulling him from his crazy thoughts.

"Sure…Hank Jr. if it's a boy, and Ashley if it's a girl."

"You sound like you've given this a lot of thought." She tilted her head slightly looked at him curiously. "I understand where the Hank Jr. came from, but what about Ashley?"

"My dad told me that my mother had always wanted two children, a Hank and an Ashley. She died before she could have an Ashley, so I figure we'll fulfill her wish."

Angela reached up and touched his cheek, her eyes flowing with the golden light that did funny things to his stomach. "Beneath all your macho posturing, you're a very nice man, Hank Riverton."

Her fingers were warm on his skin and the scent of her perfume surrounded him. Desire hit him hard and fast, the desire to make love to her, to stroke fire into her veins, the desire to unite with her as he'd never joined with another woman.

He stood abruptly. "I'll go ahead and get ready

for bed.'' He grabbed his jogging shorts, then escaped to the bathroom.

As he stood beneath a cool spray of water, he tried to figure out exactly what was going on with him. It had been a very long time since he'd felt the kind of desire he'd just experienced for Angela.

What he'd wanted to do with Angela was make love, connect with her not only physically, but mentally and spiritually as well. What he'd done with every woman he'd been with since he'd loved Sarah, was merely have sex, without thought of any other connection.

Sarah. It had been years since he'd even thought of her despite the fact that at one time she'd been his entire world. She'd been eighteen, a freshman where he was a junior in college.

He'd given Sarah everything…the pains of his past, the hopes for his future. He'd held nothing back in his absolute love for her.

He loved her brown hair, her slender shape. He'd adored the way she wrinkled her nose when she was thoughtful, how she ate her food, how she looked in sleep.

He'd begun making plans for their wedding, their life together, he'd been certain that what they'd been building would last an entire lifetime. And after four months, she'd broken up with him.

''You're too intense, Hank. I just want to have fun,'' she'd told him, breaking his heart into tiny irreparable pieces.

For his last year in college, he'd watched Sarah

have fun, dating first one young man, then another. Hank had suffered unrequited love as if he were a tragic, poetic hero. When he was finished suffering, he'd begun to have fun. And he'd been having fun ever since.

So, where did these feelings for Angela come from? he wondered as he shut off the shower and grabbed a towel. It wasn't because she reminded him of Sarah. Although they were similar physically, Angela's personality was stronger, her humor better, and her mind sharper. Hank couldn't remember having such fun with Sarah as he had with Angela.

He pulled on his jogging pants and stared thoughtfully at his reflection in the mirror. His crazy desire for Angela had to be some sort of reaction to the intensive counseling they'd received, combined with intense amount of time spent together.

He relaxed. Yes, surely that was the answer. It wasn't so much that he desired Angela, but rather the circumstances they were in were conducive to producing desire. Now that he understood his attraction to her, he could deal with it.

He just had to remember that it was a desire born in the intimacy of their surroundings and beneath Barbara's tutelage of love. Once they left Mustang, they would go back to their original positions as boss and secretary, with no emotional or physical complications.

By the time he fell asleep that night, he was secure in the fact that he felt nothing for Angela, that the brief moments of desire he experienced where she was concerned weren't true emotions, but rather manufactured by the circumstances of their enforced intimacy.

He awakened the next morning with the scent of her hair filling his head…the fragrant scent of spring flowers and fresh rain. Without opening his eyes, he knew she was once again draped across his body, her head on his chest, one of his arms trapped beneath her.

He knew she was still asleep, felt the languid, steady rhythm of her heart, the soft even breaths that warmed his chest. Her body molded against his side, warm, soft and enticing.

He opened his eyes to see that the light of dawn stole into the bedroom window, pale yellow shafts that created a cozy golden glow to the room. He gazed at Angela's sleeping countenance, wondering why he'd ever thought her plain.

Her features were strong and distinctive, arranged just unconventionally enough to be interesting…but not plain. He rubbed a strand of hair between two fingers, not wanting to awaken her, but needing to touch the shiny silk.

This is how husbands and wives all over the world awakened, he thought. In each other's arms.

And many of them would begin their day by making love to each other. It would either be a fast, passionate encounter, or a slow, languid joining. Or perhaps some of those husbands and wives would talk about their plans for the day, about what they hoped to accomplish.

It was the kind of sharing that had always frightened Hank. But, at this moment, with Angela in his arms and the dawn of a new day sifting through the curtains, it didn't seem frightening...it seemed nice.

Before he had time to fully digest his thoughts, Angela's eyes opened. For a brief moment their amber light bathed him and a smile curved the corners of her lips. In the blink of her eyes, the amber radiance disappeared, the smile fell away and she jerked to an upright position, her cheeks stained bright red.

"I'm sorry," she exclaimed as she scooted to the far side of the bed. Two buttons of her pajama top had come undone, gifting him a tantalizing glimpse of the swell of her breasts. "I didn't mean to crowd you." Her voice held her horror.

"I didn't feel crowded," he replied. His head filled with a vision of him unfastening the rest of the buttons of her top, parting the cotton material to reveal the smooth, silky skin beneath. He could almost taste her on his lips, feel the warmth of her as he caressed each inch of flesh that was bared to him.

"I don't know why I do that...I mean...maybe I sleep on that side of the bed at home...maybe I get cold in the night...I don't consciously..."

"Angela, stop. It's okay." For some reason, her profusion of protests and excuses irritated him. "I know I'm the last man on earth you'd consciously want to cuddle with.'' He got out of bed, more irritated with himself than he was with her.

He must have been having a nightmare, thinking about making love to her...sharing morning thoughts with her. That's what men did with their wives, and he didn't want a wife. And he damned straight wasn't about to get all soft and gooey over the idea of getting married just because of a week of marriage encounter workshops. What was happening to him? He had to get a grip.

He grabbed his clothes for the day and stalked into the bathroom, leaving her openmouthed and staring after him from her side of the bed.

Angela knew why Hank seemed distant and slightly irritated with her all day. It was because she'd once again sought him in sleep, curled up nearly on top of him, practically smothering him.

She didn't know what unconscious thoughts drew her to him in the darkness of the night. She wasn't in control of the magnetic energy that flowed between them while they slept. But she could understand his aggravation with her unwanted snuggling.

He remained cool and distant throughout breakfast, warming only when it was time for their private workshop with Barbara. Angela knew his warmth at that time was strictly for show, to keep the pretense of their marital state working.

"Peccadilloes,'' Barbara said once they were seated on the sofa in the library.

"I beg your pardon?" Hank said.

"Peccadilloes," Barbara repeated. "Irritating habits, aggravating quirks that drive you insane. That's what we're going to explore today."

She handed them each a small notebook and a pen. "I want you to write down the little things that your mate does that drives you insane. No-holds-barred, don't hold back."

Angela stared down at the paper, trying to think of anything Hank had done in the two days they'd been sharing their room together that might be considered irritating. Nothing specific came to mind. He'd been a thoughtful roommate, picking up after himself and not spending too long in the bathroom.

She closed her eyes, trying to visualize a day in, day out sort of existence with him. What would he do to aggravate her? What about him would irritate her to death?

She opened her eyes and looked at Hank and saw that he was writing something. She frowned. What was he writing about her? What could she have done that was aggravating to him? Was he writing that she was a bed hog? Her cheeks warmed at the thought.

Her frown deepened as she looked at her notebook again. She had to think of something. Everyone had little quirks, tiny habits that drove their mates crazy. Like squeezing the toothpaste from the middle or leaving the toilet lid up.

But, in their time together, Hank hadn't left the lid up and she didn't know how he squeezed his toothpaste since his toiletries were always picked up and put away when she went into the bathroom.

Mind racing, she started to write, realizing it didn't have to be true. Their marriage wasn't real, why did the quirks that bothered her have to be real? She smiled, beginning to enjoy the exercise.

Barbara gave them about fifteen minutes to write. "Okay, by now you should have listed the biggest offenses," she said with a smile. "Let's start with Angela. What's the first thing you wrote down?"

"He never calls when he's going to get home late from work," Angela replied, not looking at Hank. She was almost afraid to look at him for fear of bursting into giggles.

"And how does that make you feel?" Barbara asked.

Angela thought for a moment. "Like I'm not important to him. He takes me for granted." She warmed to the fantasy. "Sometimes I go all out to cook a wonderful meal. I set the table with our best china and light candles, you know, plan a wonderful romantic evening. Then he doesn't call and he doesn't come home until everything is ruined." She shot a surreptitious glance at Hank. His eyes gleamed with humor...and the warning of payback.

"Hank, do you hear what Angela is telling you? That by not calling her you make her feel as if she isn't important to you," Barbara said.

"I hear her," he replied.

"Tell her that you're sorry she feels that way."

Barbara smiled, the smile of a mother watching her children playing nice together.

Hank nodded, and reached for Angela's hand. "I'm sorry, darling. I didn't realize how my not calling made you feel. I promise to do better in the future." He squeezed her hand, a renewed promise of payback.

"Okay…good." Barbara smiled. "Now Hank, it's your turn."

"She uses sex as a weapon," he replied.

Angela gasped. "I do not," she protested.

Hank nodded solemnly. "She does," he said to Barbara. "You do," he repeated to Angela. He focused back on Barbara. "If I do or say something that makes her unhappy, she won't make love to me that night. She won't let me kiss her or hug her. I feel like there are times I have to practically beg her to get the opportunity to physically love her."

"That's ridiculous," Angela exclaimed.

Hank cast Barbara a hangdog look of sadness. "And now I probably won't be able to touch her tonight, no matter how much I yearn for her."

Barbara looked at Angela. "Is sex uncomfortable for you, either physically or emotionally?"

"No." She glared at Hank. He smiled rather sadly, giving her a wounded look. Oh, he was good. He was definitely good.

Angela gazed down at her lap, then once again directed her focus on Hank. "I'm sorry. It isn't a conscious thing to withhold myself from you. It's just when I don't feel important to you, I'm not in the mood to be with you intimately. And most of the time your work is more important than me and my needs.''

Satisfaction flooded through her as she realized how neatly she'd placed the issues back in his lap.

''So, it sounds like one of the issues you two need to work on is mutual respect,'' Barbara replied. ''Mutual respect and making sure your mate feels important. Hank, what else do you have on your list?''

''She binds her hair.''

Angela looked at him in surprise, a hand automatically shooting to the nape of her neck where her hair was tied with a pale blue scarf. ''I tie it back because it's easier than messing with it.''

''I wish you'd wear it loose. You have gorgeous hair, but you never show it off,'' Hank said. All glints of humor were gone from his eyes. Instead, Angela saw a whisper of yearning, a shimmer of truth in their dark-blue depths.

''I...I could wear it down sometimes,'' she said. The light in his eyes caused a strange, evocative warmth in the pit of her stomach.

''That's seems easy enough,'' Barbara said, drawing both Hank and Angela's attention away from each other and toward her. ''Some days you can wear it down, and other days you can pin it back. A happy compromise.'' She smiled at Angela. ''Your turn again. What else did you write down?''

Angela picked up her notebook and gazed down

at it, trying to forget that solitary moment when she'd seen those odd, unfamiliar emotions in Hank's eyes.

Surely she'd only imagined them. Uncomfortable with the sudden somber mood between herself and her pretend husband, she chose another item on her list that she thought would make him laugh.

"Sometimes he treats me like his secretary instead of his wife," she announced. "And, I can tell you for a fact he doesn't pay his secretary half what she's worth." She was relieved to see the familiar light of humor in his eyes.

The rest of the session sped by as Barbara talked to them about compromise, avoiding bad habits and how to reinforce good habits. She explained to them that it was better to talk about pet peeves than to let little irritations grow out of control. "Communication between the two of you is the key to a healthy, happy marriage," she concluded.

"I'm going to take a ride with Trent. He wants to take me over to his brother-in-law's place to see a couple of horses," Hank said after the session was finished. "We'll be back in an hour or so."

"Okay," Angela replied. Angela had a feeling his outing was less about seeing horses and more about seeing less of her.

He probably hadn't realized how long a week would be pretending to be bound to a woman he wasn't interested in. He hadn't consciously thought about how intimate it would be, sharing not only workshops geared to marital bliss, but also a bed-room…a bed.

Angela went upstairs to the bedroom. She had a couple hours to herself before dinner. She knew Stan and Edie would be in their private session with Barbara.

She sat on the edge of the bed and opened a magazine she'd packed to bring. She thumbed through the pages, but none of the articles interested her, none of the pages took her mind off her boss.

She knew what was happening. The crush she'd once had on Hank, the infatuation she'd thought had ended long ago, had returned with a vengeance.

She wasn't sure exactly when it had reap-peared…whether it had been when he'd kissed her, or during one of their sharing sessions with Bar-bara. In any case, the timing didn't matter.

Standing from the bed, she stared at the diamond ring on her finger. It sparkled as a ray of sunshine flooding through the window danced on its surface.

It was a beautiful ring, but it didn't fit quite right. Just like she and Hank didn't fit right. The ring could be sized, made smaller or larger, but she and Hank would always be a misfit. She'd do well to remember that.

It was foolish, entertaining any romantic thoughts where Hank was concerned. She knew better than anyone the kind of women he liked. She'd sent them all flowers, had ordered them gifts, had made dinner reservations at fancy restaurants for Hank and his lady of the moment.

She couldn't compete with those gorgeous, poised women, and she'd be crazy to even try. Funny face. Her dad's pet name echoed in her mind. Hank obviously liked physically beautiful women, that's all she'd ever seen him with. One after another, his love life was like a parade of contestants from a beauty pageant.

Hank might think her hair was pretty, he might say he enjoyed her sense of humor. But, that was a long way from love. Men like Hank didn't love women like Angela.

Besides, she wasn't in love with him. She just had a crush, a harmless little crush that would never evolve into anything more. She couldn't let it evolve into something deeper, because only a fool would allow her boss to break her heart.

Chapter Seven

"Whoa. Easy boy." Cameron Gallagher gentled the huge stallion with a caress on the neck.

The black stallion was enclosed in a large, wooden corral. Hank and Trent stood outside the corral, watching Trent's brother-in-law, Cameron, work with the half-wild beast. Dust rode the wind as the horse anxiously pawed the dry ground.

"He's a beauty, isn't he?" Trent observed.

"He sure is," Hank agreed.

"Cam caught him two weeks ago in a box canyon where several packs of wild horses roam," Trent explained. "He'd had his eye on that stallion for months before he actually managed to rope him."

"He's good with horses," Hank said as he watched the tall, dark-haired cowboy working with the stallion.

"Yeah, about the only things Cameron really likes are horses, his wife and his daughter...not necessarily in that order."

Trent nodded as Cameron approached where he and Hank stood. "Hey Cam."

"Trent." Cameron nodded.

"This is Hank Riverton from Great Falls. I've been telling him about your success in breaking the horses in the wild pack."

"Are you a rancher, Mr. Riverton?" Cameron asked as he shook Hank's hand.

"Not at the present time...but maybe in the future. Sometime I'd like a little place...maybe keep a couple of horses," Hank replied, surprised to realize his words were true.

"There's lots of prime land around Mustang," Cameron said.

"I'd probably be looking around the Great Falls area," Hank replied. He made a mental note to himself to check out the possibility of buying some property when he returned to Great Falls. It would be nice to have several acres, nothing too big, but enough land to keep some horses for pleasure purposes.

"Well, best of luck to you," Cameron said, obviously itching to get back to his work with the stallion.

Trent looked at his watch. "Yeah, I suppose we ought to get back. Elena and I have our session with Barbara right before dinner."

"What made you decide to do this week-long

marital enrichment thing?'' Hank asked as the two men walked back to Trent's pickup.

Trent shrugged. ''Elena thought it would be good for us.'' He cast Hank a conspiratorial wink. ''You know women, they love this bonding stuff.''

''And you didn't mind?'' Hank asked.

Trent smiled, a smile that made him appear as if he had the most fantastic secret in the world. ''Nah. I'm happy doing whatever makes her happy. This seemed to be a small enough price to pay to please her.''

An uncharacteristic surge of envy once again shot through Hank. As the two men drove back to Brody's place, Hank thought of Trent's smile. It had been more than the simple gesture of a happy man...it had been the smile of a man who'd found the secret of profound bliss...and he'd found it in the happiness of his wife.

Hank had never given much thought to marriage and family. He simply hadn't been interested before. But now he found himself contemplating the idea, trying to imagine what it would be like to love a woman every day, every night for a lifetime. What would it be like to hold a newborn Hank Jr. or a little Ashley in his arms? For the first time in forever, the idea didn't exactly scare him, but rather held a strange appeal.

Maybe it was time to start wife hunting. He was thirty-three years old. If he intended to have children he didn't want to start a family when he was too old to enjoy little ones.

"You like being a father?" he asked Trent.

Trent nodded. "If I do nothing else in my life but raise my little boy, I've done something important," he replied. Trent grinned at him knowingly. "Does your wife's pregnancy make you just a little bit nervous?"

"My wife's....oh...yeah...sort of..." The words stuttered out of Hank and for a brief moment he felt the need to come clean, to tell Trent that his marriage, Angela's pending motherhood, all of it was nothing more than a manufactured lie for business' sake.

"Don't sweat it," Trent said with a reassuring grin. "Having babies is almost as much fun as making babies."

Hank gave him a weak smile in return. The impulse to come clean passed. There was no point in telling the truth, no point in risking the Robinson account because of a momentary flare of his conscience.

When they got back to the ranch, Trent met up with Elena for their private session with Barbara, and Hank found Angela pacing in their bedroom.

"You trying to wear a hole in that rug?" he asked as he walked into the room.

"No, just thinking," she replied. She sank down on the love seat, a touch of uneasiness in her eyes. "Did you see Trent's brother-in-law's horses?"

"Some of them." Hank sat on the edge of the bed. He knew he'd left abruptly with Trent, leaving her to cool her heels here by herself.

But, somehow he felt as if all his disturbing thoughts about marriage and family revolved around the woman who sat facing him. It frightened him.

Since Angela had begun working with him two years ago, not only his business, but his life had run smoothly. She'd taken care of things for him, reminded him of not only business appointments, but personal engagements as well.

He'd had five secretaries in the year before finding Angela. He had a feeling that finding an appropriate wife would be far easier than finding a good secretary. He wasn't about to jeopardize what he had by acting out on a crazy impulse or giving into the absurd desire for her that struck him at brief intervals.

She looked especially attractive at the moment, wearing a pair of worn, tight jeans that emphasized the length of her legs, and a caramel-colored blouse that perfectly matched the golden brown of her eyes.

"So, what do you want to do before dinner? Or have you made plans to do something else?" She looked at her watch. "We've got about an hour and a half."

"You go ahead and do whatever you want." Hank stretched out on the bed. "I think I'll take a little nap." It was time to regain his distance from her, regain and maintain. He closed his eyes, far too aware of her presence in the room.

"Okay. Then I'll see you at dinner?"

He grunted a noncommitted reply. He heard her stand, felt her gaze on him as she hesitated. Then he heard her footsteps leading her out of the room.

He sighed in relief, hoping the scent of her perfume went with her rather than remained in the air to agitate him.

Four more days and they would be finished with this crazy week. Four more days and they would go back to Great Falls, back to their positions as boss and secretary.

Surely he could be smart for four days. Surely he could manage to pretend to be her husband, yet keep himself distanced enough so that he wouldn't jeopardize their future work together.

And for the next two days, Hank did manage to keep his distance. They ate each meal together, laughing and joking with the others. They attended the workshops with Barbara, talking about fears, and dreams and goals. He managed to be cordial and polite as they spent their free time with the other couples.

Hank was pleasant to Angela, played the role of happy husband, yet somehow managed to keep his emotional distance from her.

He could tell she felt his withdrawal from her. He could see questions in her eyes, but he didn't answer them. What point was there in confessing that he had the hots for his secretary? Especially since he intended to do nothing about his feelings for her.

The only time they touched was in the dead zone

of sleep. Every night, despite his resolve to the contrary, their bodies sought the warmth, the tactile
pleasure of one another. And every morning they
awakened, wrapped in each other's embrace, and
pulled apart as if burned by the contact.

By Saturday afternoon, Hank silently congratulated himself on a job well done. They had fooled
not only Brody and Barbara, but all the other couples as well and Hank had managed to put his
strange feelings for Angela behind him.

Those moments of desire, the crazy need to kiss
her, to hold her, had passed and first thing in the
morning they would be back on the road to Great
Falls, back to their normal and very separate lives.

He gave Angela a confident smile as they started
their last private workshop with Barbara. As they
had done all week long, they sat on the plush throw
rug in front of the empty fireplace as Barbara sat in
a chair some distance away from them.

"I have really enjoyed working with the two of
you this past week," Barbara said. "Next week I'll
be mailing you a short questionnaire. I hope you'll
take the time to tell me what you thought of your
experience here, what worked and didn't work to
increase your marital fulfillment."

"It's been a wonderful week for us, Barbara,"
Angela said. Hank nodded his agreement, as always
pleased by Angela's natural graciousness.

She would make some man a wonderful wife, he
thought, fighting a pang of regret. She would be an

asset to any man's life. But, he didn't want her as his wife. He desperately needed her as his secretary.

"Okay." Barbara clapped her hands together and smiled. "Today we're going to experience something fun. It doesn't take long for married people to take sex for granted. The nights of long caresses, of endless foreplay usually end quickly after the wedding vows are said."

Hank felt a nervous knot form in his stomach. What did Barbara want them to do? Indulge in intimate foreplay right here in the library...right here in front of her? Surely not. He looked at Angela, saw the anxiety that darkened her eyes. Apparently her thoughts were much like his own.

Barbara laughed. "You should see your faces. Don't worry, I'm not some voyeur intent on sharing intimate moments with you. On the contrary, I don't want you touching each other in a sexual manner at all, but I do want you to touch each other."

"What do you mean? Touch each other?" Hank tried not to radiate the apprehension he felt. Touching Angela, in any way, shape or form, had become an exquisite form of torture. He'd definitely prefer to skip this particular exercise, but there was no way he could tell that to Barbara.

"Okay, Hank. We'll start with you. I want you to explore Angela's face with your hands." Barbara looked at him expectantly.

Hank looked at Angela, wondering if anyone else in the room could hear the thunderous beat of his heart. He didn't want to touch her...because he wanted desperately to touch her.

He framed her face with his hands, then looked at Barbara. "I'm not sure what you want me to do," he said.

"Close your eyes. Pretend that the only way you can see her is through your fingertips," Barbara instructed. "Start with her hair, then work your way down all the features of her face."

Hank closed his eyes, his fingers working to untie the scarf that held her hair at the nape of her neck. As the scarf came undone, her hair sprang free and he tangled his hands in the length of it.

The silky strands felt wonderfully erotic against his palms, across the back of his hands. He realized he'd dreamed of doing just this...luxuriating in her beautiful hair, ever since he'd seen it loose and flowing around her shoulders on the morning he'd picked her up at her house.

He left her hair and smoothed his fingertips across her forehead, over her perfectly arched eyebrows and down the length of her nose. Her skin was smooth, softer than Hank had ever imagined.

Her cheeks were warm, her lips warmer and when Hank's fingertips danced lightly across her lips, he opened his eyes and looked at her.

Why had he ever believed her to be plain? Her amber eyes shone with a brilliance that stole his breath away. Long, gold-tipped lashes cast faint shadows as she broke his eye contact with a self-conscious blush.

And then it was her turn to examine his features. Her fingertips were cold and trembled slightly as she stroked across his brow and down his cheeks. When her fingers touched his mouth, he felt the fire that had been simmering in the pit of his stomach burst into flame.

He felt her breath on his face. Warm and sweet, her breaths came a little faster, a little deeper than normal, letting him know that she, too, was affected on some primal level by this exercise of touch.

"Okay," Barbara's voice broke the spell. Angela pulled her hands away from him and Hank drew a deep, steadying breath.

"Now your hands," Barbara said. "I want you to explore each other's hands."

Again Hank's heart pumped erratically in his chest. He wanted out…away from here, away from Angela. But, instead of jumping up and leaving, instead of making any sort of scene, he reached out for her hands.

Small. Dainty. Hank had never known that hands could be so damned erotic. Her fingers warmed as their hands clasped, reclasped, entangled and enfolded each other.

"I have one last assignment for the two of you," Barbara said after several moments had passed. Hank released Angela's hand, grateful for the interruption.

"Tonight, I'd like for the two of you to explore each other's bodies. I want you to touch and caress everywhere except the usual sexual places. Arms…

legs…knees…shoulders…I want you both to realize that making love isn't just about touching sex organs. Take the time to discover those secret erogenous zones you each have. And that's it.'' Barbara stood.

Hank shot up from the throw rug as if he'd been kicked up from some invisible foot. Angela also rose to her feet, her cheeks flaming a brilliant red that matched the T-shirt she wore.

''I'll see you both at dinner,'' Barbara said. With a nod and a smile, she left the two of them alone in the library.

''Well,'' Hank said, forcing a lighthearted smile. ''That was certainly intense,'' he said.

''A little too intense for me,'' Angela said, her gaze not meeting his. ''That's one homework assignment we won't be completing.''

Remorse shot through Hank. As Angela started to leave the library, he caught her arm. ''Angela, I'm sorry. I had no idea what I was getting us into when I hatched this scheme.''

She stepped away from him and shrugged. ''It's all right.''

''Yeah, but you didn't exactly agree to being pawed by me when you agreed to be my wife.'' He searched her face, looking for an indication that she wasn't angry, that it would be all right. ''I need to know that we can put this all behind us when we get back to the office,'' he finally said.

''Of course we can,'' she said, although her gaze still didn't meet his.

"Are you sure?"

She finally looked at him, her eyes calm and clear. "There's no problem, Hank. When we get back to the office, the ring comes off my finger, you go back to being Mr. Riverton, and I get a bonus that makes it all worthwhile."

Hank felt a curious disappointment at the mention of the bonus, although he had no idea where the disappointment came from. He'd known all along she was going along with the marriage conspiracy for bonus money.

Her smiles, her laughter, even the kiss they'd shared had all been part of a role...a role to help him maintain the Robinson account and win her a big bonus check. The bottom line was that their entire pretend marriage was all about money. For just a moment he'd almost forgotten that fact.

"If you don't mind, I think I'll lie down for a little while before dinner. I have a headache," she said.

Hank smiled. "Our first headache," he said, trying to find the humor that had guided them through the past five days.

"I guess so," she agreed, but there was no responding smile, no glint of humor lighting her eyes. Without saying anything else, she turned and left the room.

When she was gone, Hank sank down on one of the chairs, wondering why in the world he felt so low. They'd made it through the week, pulled the wool over everyone's eyes. He'd retain the Robinson account and when they got back to Great Falls, nothing would be different than it had been before. So, why did he feel so bad?

Angela dressed in her pajamas, grateful that tonight was the very last night she would sleep in a bed with Hank Riverton. Tonight was the last night they would pretend a relationship that didn't exist, that would never exist.

She was relieved that the experience was almost over, relieved that by this time tomorrow she'd be back in her own bed, at home with her mother and Brian.

Making sure her pajama top was buttoned up, she turned away from the bathroom mirror. She'd been in here long enough that Hank had probably already fallen asleep.

He was probably relieved that the week was almost over, too. The first couple of days they'd been here, the game had been almost fun. Hank had teased and joked with her, they'd talked and she'd learned more about him. Then, he'd clammed up, stopped teasing and grown distant. She didn't know exactly what had caused his change, but she suspected it was their kiss.

He'd probably withdrawn to make sure she didn't get any crazy ideas that he cared about her. He'd probably been afraid she'd somehow believe their little game of make-believe, afraid that the poor, little plain secretary would become delusional.

She left the bathroom and went into the bedroom,

where Hank appeared to be sound asleep. She shut off the bedside lamp, then crawled onto the bed with her back facing Hank. Every night she clung to her side of the bed as if hanging from a precipice and every night when she fell asleep, she fell into the middle of the bed and Hank's arms.

The room was silent, except for the sound of their breathing. Angela closed her eyes and tried to still her mind so sleep could overtake her, but her mind refused to be still.

All she could think about was the exercise Barbara had led them through that afternoon. Touching Hank's face, exploring his handsome features with the tips of her fingers had created a wave of desire inside her...a desire she'd never felt before.

She'd looked into his eyes and had wanted to drown in the midnight-blue depths. For the rest of the day she'd felt as if she were in water over her head, making it difficult to breath, impossible to focus on anything else but Hank.

"Angela?"

His deep voice startled her. For a split second she thought of not answering, of pretending she was asleep.

"Are you asleep?"

"No," she finally answered and rolled over on her back.

He was on his side, facing her. He braced himself with his elbow and gazed at her, his eyes silvery in the moonlit room. "I'm thinking about buying some land when we get back to Great Falls," he said. "Nothing major, just enough for a house, a barn and a couple of horses."

Angela turned over and faced him in surprise. "What about your business?"

"Oh, nothing will change there, except maybe I'll start working less hours, give myself a little more free time." He turned over on his back and stared up at the ceiling. "I've been doing a lot of thinking in the last couple of days." He plumped his pillow beneath his head, his gaze thoughtful.

"Thinking about what?" Angela asked.

"The day I watched them auction off our land, our belongings, I swore that I'd work hard enough, get rich enough that nobody would ever take from me again." He turned back to look at her. "I realize now that I could have lost the Robinson account and the business would have been fine."

"Are you telling me that this entire week wasn't really necessary?" she asked.

"For the reasons I originally told you, no." He was silent for a moment. "But maybe necessary for other reasons. Without this week, I wouldn't have realized that I've been driving myself so hard I've lost track of my original goal."

"And what was your original goal?" Angela asked. Their voices were soft. It felt oddly intimate, lying next to him, whispering together in the darkness of the night.

"Happiness." Hank drew a deep breath. "When I first started the agency, my plan was to get enough money to buy some land and get a horse like the one I lost. Yes, as soon as we get back, I'm going to buy me a nice ranch house with a couple of acres." His eyes gleamed with anticipation.

"It should be a house with a big front porch," Angela said, easily able to envision such a place.

"Yeah…a front porch big enough for a swing or a glider so I can sit and watch the sun set each evening."

"Or enjoy your first cup of morning coffee as you watch the sunrise," Angela added.

Hank nodded, a soft smile curving his lips. "The barn has to be a traditional red, and the house will have a white wooden fence around the immediate yard."

"With flowers planted everywhere, blooming at various times of the year."

"It's going to be great," he said.

"Sounds perfect," she agreed with a touch of wistfulness, wishing it could be their shared dream, instead of just his own. But she had to remember, he wasn't talking about her sharing in his dreams, in his future.

"It's what I've always wanted…what I lost track of. I figured eventually I'd get married, then have some kids. And I'd be successful enough that my children would never know what it was like to lose a home."

The thought of Hank marrying somebody, setting up a family on a little piece of land, filled Angela with a wistful yearning. "That's nice, Hank. I hope you reach your goal." She hoped he didn't notice that her voice was deeper, fuller than usual.

"If I do, it will be because of you. If you hadn't agreed to come with me this week, then I wouldn't have realized how off course I've gotten. This week and you have reminded me of all the things I want in life. And for that, I thank you." Before she knew his intention, he leaned forward and kissed her.

Chapter Eight

His kiss didn't surprise her so much, but his hunger did. His mouth covered hers with intense heat, with ravenous need, at the same time he moved closer and wrapped his arms around her.

She had no time to prepare for the overwhelming onslaught, no time to arm herself against the sensual assault of his embrace, the utter possession of his kiss.

As his tongue danced and tangled with hers, desire washed over her, through her...a desire she'd never experienced before, desire that made rational thought nearly impossible.

He rolled over on his back, bringing her with him so that she half lay on his chest. Still, he claimed her lips with his, the deep kiss continuing as his hands moved up and down her back.

Angela felt as if she had plunged into a dream. A dream of passion, and love...and Hank. Her head spun with the magic of his touch. She felt her blood heating inside her veins, her body electrifying as his kiss lingered on and on.

After several stroking motions on top of her pajama top, his hands moved beneath, caressing her bare back with his fevered movements. Every place his hands and fingers touched sang with pleasure.

Angela smoothed her hands over his bare chest and shoulders, feeling the strength, the sinewy muscle that lay beneath his skin. She loved the way his flesh felt, the way his chest hairs curled and sprang around her fingers. Never had she touched a male so boldly, and never had she felt so utterly female.

With a deep groan, Hank rolled them over again, this time so he was fully on top of her. Angela had never been in such an intimate position with a man, and the spinning of her mind intensified, whirling with dizzy intoxication as she felt his desire for her.

He moved his mouth from hers, and instead kissed across her cheeks, along her jaw and finally down the length of her neck. Angela gasped with sheer pleasure as his lips nipped and teased.

His lips found the sensitive place behind her ear. His rapid breaths spoke of his desire for her and increased her delight. As his mouth moved down her neck, sweetly teasing her with fiery kisses, she tangled her hands in the thick of his hair and a soft moan escaped her.

His hands moved up and down her back, then

slid down her sides, lingering momentarily on the swell of each breast. Angela closed her eyes, knowing they should stop, she should stop him, but not wanting to halt what had seemed destined to happen since the moment she'd agreed to be his pretend wife.

As his hands finally touched her breasts, she moaned with pleasure. Once more his mouth possessed hers, drinking deeply as his hands cupped her breasts, his fingertips rolling across their hardened peaks.

Again he rolled them over so she was beneath him. He broke the kiss and looked down at her. His eyes glittered darkly, hypnotically as one by one, he unfastened the buttons on her pajama top.

Angela didn't move. She was transfixed by the desire she saw in his eyes, enthralled by the contagious fever that seemed to engulf them both. She wanted him to look at her like this forever. When he gazed at her with such want, such need, she felt like the most beautiful woman in the world. She wanted to feel his hands on her, his lips on her forever.

"I want you," he said as he unfastened the last button. He didn't move the material aside, instead he continued to hold her gaze, as if giving her a chance to stop him now, before things reeled out of control.

"Say my name," she whispered breathlessly, needing to know that he was seeing her, wanting her, not some fantasy woman in his head.

She felt as if she were in a dream, but she wanted to make certain that he was not. "Please, say my name...say it."

"Angela. Angela." Her name sang from his lips. "My sweet Angela. I want you."

She'd believed she would never hear those words from a man. She'd never believed she would ever inspire great desire, that any man would ever say her name with such barely controlled passion.

As her gaze remained locked with his, she moved the material that covered her, exposing her breasts to him.

"Sweet Angela," he whispered, then bent his head and kissed first her lips, then her neck, then he captured the tip of one of her breasts with his mouth.

Desire, sharp and intense, swept through Angela, a novel emotion that both frightened and electrified her. She wrapped her arms around him, smoothing her palms down the width of his back. She could feel the taut muscles beneath, felt the heat that emanated from his skin, a heat she wanted to crawl into forever.

His hips moved against hers, an intimate rhythm that created a well of want inside her. Her hips matched his rhythm, unable to do anything but respond. She felt his heartbeat, a frantic flutter that matched her own as they moved sensually together.

She'd never felt the sensations her body felt at this moment...wild desire, crazed excitement and still more than a little touch of fear.

He was taking her where she'd never been. He was evoking in her sensations she'd never, ever felt. She felt like a comet, careening out of control, a meteorite burning itself up.

It wasn't until Hank's fingers touched the waistband of her pajama bottoms that the fear grew to mammoth proportions, overwhelming the incredible desire and excitement.

"Hank..." Her voice was a bare whisper, almost inaudible against their frantic breathing, their gasps of desire. "Hank...I lied," she finally blurted.

He stopped moving, seemed to stop breathing for a long, infinite moment. "What?"

Angela drew a gulp of air. "I lied...when I told you I've had lovers before. It wasn't true. I've never had a lover...never."

"You mean you're a....you haven't..." He rolled off her and onto his back. For a moment neither of them said anything as they waited for blood to cool, for heartbeats to slow.

Angela pulled her top together and fastened the buttons, her fingers trembling with residual desire. She waited for him to speak, unsure what more to say.

On one hand, she was grateful that they'd stopped before actually making love. On the other hand, she was left with an ache of hollow need, a need she knew instinctively only one man would have been able to fill...Hank.

She loved him. What had begun as a harmless crush so long ago, had somehow blossomed in the last week into real, and abiding love. The realization struck her like a thousand-pound weight attaching to her heart.

"Angela...I'm sorry." He finally spoke, and his words spiraled down inside her, adding additional weight to her overburdened heart. "I don't know what to say..."

"Please. Don't say anything," she replied, tears burning at her eyes. "It's my fault as much as it is yours. I should never have let things get so out of control. Let's just say that we both almost made a grave mistake and leave it at that." She heard his sigh and recognized it as a huge sigh of relief.

"Okay," he replied after another long moment of silence. "I'm sure it's just a matter of these crazy circumstances," he said, as if needing a logical explanation for their near lovemaking. "I mean... we've pretended we're married, we've been sharing the same bed..."

"I'm sure you're right," she replied, wanting him to stop with the excuses and hoping he didn't hear the stinging heartache in her voice.

They lay side by side, neither speaking for several long moments. The moonlight peeked in the window, illuminating the room in a silvery glow.

She knew if she turned over and looked at him she'd be able to see his features. She'd be able to see the face, all the features that made up the man she loved.

"Good night," he finally said, then turned away from her.

"Good night," Angela whispered. She turned her back to him, tears seeping from beneath her eyelids.

Her love for him ached inside her, not just a physical need, but a need much bigger, much more profound.

She loved him and knew not in a million years, would he ever love her back. Men like Hank Riverton didn't fall in love with women like Angela Samuels, and women like Angela Samuels were fools if they allowed themselves to fall in love with men like Hank Riverton.

She'd felt beautiful for those brief moments in his arms, but reality stared at her each morning in the mirror. Reality was in her father's words of long ago.

Fool, a tiny voice yelled at her. How could you have let this happen? She stared at the wall, trying to think of the defining moment when a simple, harmless crush had turned to something deeper, when he'd managed to become more than her boss, more than a friend.

It was impossible to identify any singular moment. Love had come from laughter, through respect, despite differences. Love had climbed around barriers, embraced similarities and grown into something too big for her to avoid or ignore.

She wasn't sure when Hank finally fell asleep. He tossed and turned for at least an hour, then finally grew silent, his breathing pattern letting her know he'd found the peace of slumber.

When she thought he was finally soundly sleeping, she turned back over and found herself looking at the face of the man she loved.

In the past week she'd grown intimately familiar with his face. Her fingers held the sensory memory of touching the tiny wrinkles that radiated out from his eyes, the slight hollow of his cheeks, the soft curve of his mouth. Her head was filled with a million memories of his features...laughing, thoughtful, shamefaced and tender.

She rolled over on her back and touched her stomach. How she wished she was carrying his child, his little Hank Jr. or Ashley. How wonderful it must be to carry a seed of love that blossomed into a baby.

With a deep sigh, she turned, once again turning away from Hank. She stared at the wall until dawn light cast shadows and the sound of morning drifted through the window. She made sure that she didn't fall asleep, that her traitorous body didn't get an opportunity to end up in his arms.

Twice in his sleep, he reached for her and twice she evaded him by moving aside, gently pushing him back. It would have been easy to allow a sleepy embrace to occur, but Angela knew it would only make her heartbreak deeper than it already was.

She pretended to be sleeping when she felt Hank stir and knew he had awakened. Despite the fact that her back was to him, she felt him looking at her, felt the warmth of his gaze on her back. After a long moment, he got out of bed and disappeared into the bathroom.

Angela rolled over on her back and rubbed her gritty eyes. She'd shed few tears throughout the night, although she felt as if a million rested just behind her eyelids, ready to burst free at any given moment. But she refused to release them here, with him lying in the bed next to her.

She tried to tell herself he wasn't worth crying over, that he was opinionated, selfish, conceited... all the things she wouldn't want in a man. But, she knew better. Yes, he was firm in his beliefs. But, she knew he wasn't selfish, knew he wasn't conceited. He was self-confident, secure in the man he was, but had the wonderful ability to laugh at himself.

Rubbing her eyes once again, she knew what she had to do, knew there was no alternative. She waited until they ate breakfast and said their goodbyes to the other couples and to Brody and Barbara.

She waited until they had driven several hours. They small-talked, then stopped and had lunch. Finally, when they were only miles from Great Falls she decided the time was right and there was no way to get around it.

"Hank," she began, hoping he couldn't see the emotion that crowded her heart shining from her eyes.

He cast her a quick smile. "Yeah?"

The smile pierced through her, making her ache even more, but strengthening her resolve for what she was about to do.

She drew a deep breath. "I'm officially giving

you my two-week notice," she said. "I'm quitting my job as your secretary."

Hank stomped on the brakes, causing the car behind them to honk several short, angry, blaring beeps. "What?" Surely he'd heard her wrong. She couldn't have said what he thought she'd said.

"I'm quitting my job. I'm giving you two weeks' notice," she repeated.

"What are you talking about?" he asked, trying to focus on driving and staring at her at the same time. He finally decided he couldn't do both. With a wrench of the steering wheel, he pulled to the side of the highway and squealed to a halt.

For a long moment he stared at her, willing her to take the words back, but she faced him down, a touch of defiance in her golden gaze. "Jeez, Angela. What brought this on?" He swept a hand through his hair and leaned back against the seat, shocked to distraction.

"Nothing brought this on," she protested. "It's something I've been thinking about for some time."

"Is this about last night?" He saw the flames of color that instantly lit her cheeks. "It is, isn't it?" He hit the steering wheel with the palm of his hand. "Dammit, I told you I was sorry, that it shouldn't have happened."

He rubbed his temple, where a headache had begun to pound. It was his fault. They had almost made a horrid mistake last night and it had been all his fault.

He'd intended to give her a sweet chaste kiss of thanks, but the moment his lips had touched hers, chaste had gone out of his head.

"This has nothing to do with last night," she replied. "How egotistical of you to assume that it has anything to do with last night." The words shot out of her, crisp and curt.

"Then what?" Again he raked a hand through his hair and eyed her frantically. She couldn't be serious. Maybe she had a warped sense of humor that she'd never displayed before this moment in time.

She sighed and stared out the window for a long moment, then looked back at him. "Hank, I'm tired of working for you. I'm tired of ordering your sandwiches, of picking up your dry cleaning. I'm tired of buying your father his birthday present and fetching flowers for your woman of the moment. When you hired me, you didn't tell me I'd be a combination mother/secretary/wife. When you hired me you said you'd be training me in the field of advertising."

"It will be different when we get back," Hank said, desperation filling his stomach, crushing his chest. He had to change her mind. He had to. "I told you we'd make changes when we got back, and we will." He couldn't imagine the office without her. She was the glue that held the office together. "Angela, I swear it will be different. I'll get somebody else to do those things, I'll hire you an assistant, so you have more time to work on accounts.''

''I don't believe you,'' she said flatly.

''What do you mean, you don't believe me?'' he asked incredulously. ''Why should you not believe me?''

Her eyes widened with utter disbelief. ''You just spent a week lying to people about my relationship to you. I've had seven days to see what a good liar you are.''

''That was different. I'm not lying now,'' Hank protested, a rising panic making his voice louder than he'd intended.

''Well, I don't want to work for you anymore,'' she yelled back, matching him tone for tone.

Hank drew a deep breath of air, trying to calm himself down, fighting against the absolute panic that coursed through him. He could tell by the look on her face that, at least for the moment, she was adamant. He also knew there was no point in arguing with her...at least not here and now.

''The only way I'll accept your resignation is if you type it up and present it properly in my office on Monday morning,'' he finally said.

''Fine,'' she replied. She turned her gaze out the side window.

Hank looked at her for a long moment, searching his mind for ways to change hers. Angela quit? Impossible. She was the best damned secretary he'd ever had. He wasn't about to let her slip away so easily. He put the car into gear and pulled away from the curb and back into traffic.

Within minutes they had reached Angela's home. He parked in the driveway and shut off the engine. He turned in the seat to face her. "Angela, please reconsider what you're doing." She shook her head, her resolution evident in the tightness of her features. "You have the rest of the day. All I'm asking is that you think about it."

She nodded curtly. "Okay, I'll think about it. But, I'm not going to change my mind."

Hank sighed, stunned at the idea of working without her. She didn't wait for him to say anything further. She got out of the car and opened the back door and grabbed her suitcase.

Hank quickly left the car and took the heavy bag from her. "I swear things will be different, if you'll just give me a chance," he said as he walked with her to the front door. He set her suitcase down on the porch and gazed at her pleadingly.

"Hank, don't make this more difficult than it already is," she said softly.

"If it's difficult, then it must be wrong," he exclaimed. "Angela, I need you. You keep the office running smoothly, you keep things sane."

"Goodbye, Hank," she said as she grabbed her suitcase and opened the door. "I'll see you tomorrow."

He stood on the porch long after she'd disappeared and closed the door behind her. He fought the impulse to beat down the door, climb through

a window and confront her again. He'd give her a
raise, shorten her hours...whatever it took, he had
to figure out a way to keep her.

He got back into his car, but instead of heading
to his apartment, he drove to his father's house. A
year ago, when his father Harris had remarried, he'd
also retired and bought a modest two-bedroom
home with enough backyard for a huge garden.

After parking in his father's driveway, instead of
going to the front door, Hank walked around the
side, to the back of the house where he knew he'd
probably find his dad and his stepmother, Iris.

Sure enough, Iris sat at an umbrella table sipping
a glass of iced tea, and Hank's father stood amid
the high tomato plants, plucking ripened vegetables
and putting them in a basket. It was an idyllic scene
and for some reason it irritated Hank.

"What a pleasant surprise," Iris greeted him.
"Harris, look who's here."

Harris Riverton looked up and his features
wreathed with a smile. "Hey, son." With quick,
determined strides, Harris approached. Setting his
basket on the table, he patted Hank on the back.
"We tried to get in touch with you Thursday night
to see if you wanted to meet for dinner."

"I've been out of town all week on business,"
Hank replied. His dad gestured him into an empty
seat at the table. He sat, unsure exactly what had
prompted this spontaneous visit.

"How about some iced tea?" Iris asked.

Hank nodded. "That sounds great," he agreed.

As Iris left to go into the house, Hank turned his attention to his father. Harris Riverton had always been a distinguished-looking man, with silvered temples and the trim fit of a man half his age.

At the moment, clad in a pair of worn jeans and a crisply ironed short-sleeved dress shirt, he still looked distinguished, but he also looked relaxed…happier than Hank had ever seen. Happiness…Hank had never felt more unhappy in his life than he did at the moment.

"You look good, Dad. I swear you're getting younger every day."

"Contentment, it's like the fountain of youth," Harris said.

"I wouldn't know about that," Hank replied with a sigh.

"Problems?"

Hank nodded, but said no more as Iris reappeared. Harris smiled at his wife as she handed them each their drinks, then turned his attention back to Hank. "What's up, son?"

"Is there a problem, Hank?" Iris asked. She and his father exchanged glances.

Hank released a small burst of laughter. "The way you two are looking at each other, I feel like I'm about ten years old and just got caught with a stack of naughty magazines."

Iris and Harris smiled at one another, and Hank's irritation returned full force. When they looked at each other and smiled, it was the same kind of gesture that Trent had, the one that said they were lucky, that they'd found something special and wonderful in each other.

"Hank, I wasn't around when you were growing up, but I can bet you were never the kind of boy that needed naughty magazines," Iris said with a small blush.

Hank grinned, the grin slowly fading. "My secretary is going to hand me her two-week notice tomorrow, and I don't know what I'm going to do," he said.

"You'll hire another one," Harris replied.

"It's not that simple," Hank protested. "Angela is something special."

"Then it might take you a couple tries before you hire one as good as her," Harris replied.

Hank frowned. "No...you're missing the point. Angela is truly special. She makes me laugh and she stimulates my mind. She keeps me on my toes and makes me be a better person. There's no way I can live without her in my life."

Iris eyed Hank with a small smile. "I thought we were talking about a secretary."

"We are...I am," Hank replied.

Iris's smile grew wider. "You didn't tell us you were in love with Angela."

"In love? That's ridiculous," Hank scoffed.

"Sounds like love to me," Harris replied.

Hank's heart thudded loudly as he thought of the words he'd just spoken. Angela. A picture of her face superimposed itself in his mind...the golden light of her eyes, the beauty of her smile, her infectious laughter.

He thought of her quick mind, her gentle smile, how she'd looked when she'd spoken of her love for her brother, the emptiness she'd expressed when she'd spoken of her father.

Hank loved her.

The realization hit him hard in the gut. Somehow, someway, in the past week, he'd fallen in love with his secretary. He stared at Iris, then at his father, stunned by the revelation of his heart.

Iris laughed. "You look like a deer caught in a truck's headlights."

"It was bound to happen sooner or later," Harris observed with a smile. "Face it, my boy. You sound like a man who is in love."

"But…but this wasn't supposed to happen," Hank protested. He wasn't supposed to fall in love.

He realized now that's why he'd chosen the women he had to date…because they were safe. He knew there was no way his heart would get involved with the beautiful, but shallow women he picked as companions.

"You can't pick the time that love will find you," Harris said. "I loved your mother very much, Hank. And when she died, I swore I'd never give my heart to another woman. I was afraid. I didn't want to have that kind of hurt again."

He reached over and touched Iris's hand and in that simple touch Hank saw lasting love and enduring commitment. "Then Iris came along and for the first time I knew that she was worth the risk of having my heart hurt again.''

Hank nodded thoughtfully. Is that what he had done? When Sarah had hurt his heart so many years ago, had he made a subconscious decision to never put his heart at risk again? Probably, he decided.

But it didn't matter anymore. He was in love with Angela. He'd deal with her not being his secretary any longer, but he couldn't imagine spending the rest of his life without her.

He looked at his father and Iris. ''So, what do I do now?''

Harris smiled. ''I say you go for it. Tell her you love her. I promise you the risk is worth it. And if you don't take the risk, you'll always wonder.''

A few minutes later Hank left, more confused than he'd been before he'd arrived. He loved Angela. And she intended to quit her job on Monday.

He had no idea what she thought of him, if she had any positive feelings at all for him. She'd told him on their first day as pretend husband and wife that he was selfish, egotistical and conceited. Did she still believe that?

Had the week in Mustang changed her mind where he was concerned? Evidently not, he thought with a sharp pang to his heart. After all, she planned to completely walk out of his life in two weeks' time.

As Hank drove into his apartment building parking lot, he knew what he had to do. He had two weeks to change her mind, two weeks to make her fall in love with him. And when Hank Riverton went after something, he didn't stop until he got what he wanted.

Chapter Nine

Roses. Bright red, with huge blossoms. That's the first thing Angela saw when she arrived in her office on Monday morning. The vase of blooms set centered on her desk blotter, a fragrant, vivid greeting that did nothing to cheer her.

If Hank Riverton thought she'd change her mind about continuing to work for him just because he'd bought her a dozen flowers, then he had another think coming.

Angela had spent several hours on Sunday with the classified ads from the paper spread out in front of her. She'd circled the job possibilities with red ink...red circles of heartbreak.

She couldn't believe she'd been so stupid, so vulnerable as to fall so completely, so totally for Hank's charm. The crush she'd entertained months earlier now seemed sophomoric and superficial when compared to the depth of her feelings for him now.

It wasn't that just physically he'd overwhelmed her. What she felt for him had far more depth than mere physical attraction. Her love went deep and strong, a love for the entire man, physically, spiritually, emotionally.

He made her laugh, he made her think. He challenged her yet comforted her. He was all that she had ever wanted, and she knew he was the man she would never have.

She picked up the vase of roses and held it over her trash can. If he saw them in the garbage then he would see how effective his ploy had been.

How extravagant, how like him, to go over the top in an effort to get what he wanted. But, with the fragrant scent wafting in the air and the roses' dewy perfection so exquisite to see, she couldn't throw them away. Instead she placed the vase on top of the metal file cabinet behind her desk where people coming into the office would admire them, but she couldn't see them as she sat and worked.

Her first order of the day was to call some employment agencies and set up interviews with prospective secretaries. From the moment she'd realized she loved him, she knew there was no way she could work for him, watch him date and get on with his life. But, she wasn't going to leave him in the lurch, either. She had to hire a decent replacement for herself.

She sank down at her desk and stared at the picture of Hank on the opposite wall. How on earth was she going to sit here for the next two weeks with his handsome visage a mere glance away?

She punched on her computer terminal, deciding she'd just have to keep busy, keep her attention away from the picture, away from the emotions that churned in her heart. Fourteen days…that's all she had to endure.

Surely the excitement of starting a new job, meeting new co-workers, rising to new work challenges would keep her mind off love and romance and Hank.

As she tried desperately to reassure herself of this, Hank opened his office door and stepped out. "Oh…you're here," he said.

He looked as handsome as she'd ever seen him. Clad in a navy blazer and slacks, with a starched white shirt beneath the blazer, he looked crisp and clean…and sexy as hell. The blue of the jacket emphasized the depth of that same color in his eyes…eyes that gazed around, obviously looking for the roses. He finally spied them atop the file cabinet, but his features revealed nothing.

"I told you I'd be here this morning as usual," Angela replied, then drew in a steadying breath. Why did he have to look so good? Why did she have to love him so? Why couldn't she have fallen in love with some nice, ordinary man? Why did it have to be Hank who had captured her heart?

"Could you come in here for a moment or two?" He gestured to his private, inner office.

Angela nodded and pulled her resignation notice from her purse. She'd typed it up the day before, prepared to place it on his desk first thing this morning.

She followed him into his inner sanctum. He closed the door behind them, but didn't sit down behind his desk as he usually did.

"We need to talk," he said. He took a step toward her.

She was aware of the racing of her heart. Couldn't he hear it? Couldn't he hear that it was frantically beating out her love for him? He stood too close to her and his nearness battered at her mental defenses.

"Did you want me to take a letter? Make an appointment?" Angela was grateful her voice remained cool and controlled, not showing the emotions that raged inside her.

"Did you read the card that was on the roses?" he asked.

He took another step closer, completely invading her personal space and forcing her to take a step backward. His scent, the one she had become so familiar with over the past week, filled her senses and she wanted to weep.

"No. But I'm sure it says that you want me to keep my job." She held out her notice of resignation. "Here's my answer."

He took the note and scanned it, then wadded it

up into a ball. Angela frowned. "It doesn't matter what you do with it. I've given you my notice, and that's that," she exclaimed.

"Angela, just listen to me." He approached closer, and she stepped back once again, stopping when she hit the closed door behind her. He raised his arms and placed his hands on the door on either side of her, effectively trapping her in place.

"The card on the roses didn't say anything about the job. It didn't plead with you not to quit." His eyes bore into hers, intense in a way she'd never seen before.

She was self-consciously aware of the fact that she'd put on little makeup that morning, that her hair was probably its usual curly mess, and that the gray suit she wore did nothing to compliment her.

"Angela, you should have read the card. It says that I love you."

Her heart seemed to stop for a long moment, then a deep, piercing ache set in. She stared at him, unable to believe what he'd just said.

Anger swelled up inside her. She swallowed against it, but it refused to go away. Instead it grew to mammoth proportions, overwhelming her. With one swift movement, she dunked beneath his arm and turned back to face him.

"You would do anything to get what you want, wouldn't you?" Her voice rang with condemnation. "How low you are, Hank Riverton. How low to pretend to love me so I'll agree to remain working for you."

"No." Hank looked horrified. "No, that's not it at all," he protested.

"How convenient," she continued angrily. "How convenient that you've suddenly discovered this newfound love for me at the same time I've handed you my resignation."

She shoved him out of the way and grabbed the doorknob. "I should have known that you'd try anything to get me to stay, but I never dreamed you'd sink this low." She opened the door. "I'm going to lunch," she exclaimed.

"Lunch? But, it's only a little after nine," he sputtered.

"So, fire me," she snapped back. She slammed the door behind her and grabbed her purse from her desk. As she left the building, she wondered how on earth she could have let herself fall in love with such an unethical oaf.

His bogus confession of love ached inside her, pierced her heart with a pain that took her breath away. She walked to a nearby diner where she ate lunch every day.

Of course he would have no idea how his phony love confession would hurt because he had no idea that she truly loved him.

She took her usual stool at the counter and ordered a breakfast platter and coffee, although the last thing she felt like doing was eating.

While she waited for her food to arrive, she sipped her coffee, wondering why fate had been so cruel to her. She'd only loved three men in her entire life. Her brother, Brian, her father...and Hank.

If she were Attila the Hun, she knew Brian would love her. She'd practically raised him. She'd been the one who had attended school meetings, taken him to Cub Scout functions and baseball games. She and Brian had a bond that nothing and nobody would ever break.

But when her father had left, she'd been absolutely devastated. He had been her hero, the most important man in her life and she'd never, ever in her life, understand how he'd so easily walked away.

Now that she considered it, she realized Hank and her father had a lot in common. Angela's dad had been handsome to distraction, able to charm both men and women alike.

Like Hank, Angela's dad had been ambitious. As an insurance salesman, he'd been a hustler, aggressively going after new accounts.

When he'd walked away from the marriage... from Angela, he'd taken half her heart with him. And now Hank had stolen the other half, leaving nothing left inside her chest except a hollow emptiness.

Hank had told Angela he loved her and she'd gone to lunch. But, the utter absurdity of the situation didn't make Hank laugh at all.

After she'd gone, he sank down at his desk and leaned back in his chair. He knew he'd been wrong to dupe Brody and Barbara and the other couples in Mustang. He'd known it was wrong and he'd done it anyway, and now he was paying the price.

How could he convince Angela his love was real when she'd seen him lying without a blink of his eyes? How could he gain credibility with her when he'd sacrificed it for business' sake?

He had to do something. He couldn't just sit here and let the woman he wanted to spend the rest of his life with get away.

Lunch. She'd gone to lunch. He'd find her, proclaim his love again…and again…and again…until she'd have to believe him.

He couldn't believe that she didn't somehow, someway care about him. They'd shared too many intimate moments for him to believe she was completely inured to him. He'd kissed her…but she'd kissed him back. Surely she'd kissed him because she felt something for him.

With a renewed confidence, he locked up the office and stepped outside, only to frown in confusion. Hell, she'd been his secretary for two years and he didn't know where she went for lunch.

Had she driven or walked? To the left of his office building were several drive-through services offering the standard fare of fast food. To the right were several restaurants, one a diner, another one a high-price Italian place.

The diner, Hank decided. He strode with quick, determined strides down the sidewalk, his heart racing in anticipation. He had to make her understand.

Somehow, someway he had to make her believe him.

He entered the diner and looked around, his heart thudding the beat of love as he saw her at the counter. For a long moment he stood just inside the door and watched her.

Why had it taken him so long to notice her? A week ago he hadn't been able to bring her features to mind, and now he couldn't imagine forgetting anything about her. Where had his head been for the past two years?

She stared down at her plate, moving food from one side to the other with her fork. He noticed the graceful curve of her neck, the prim position of her legs pressed tightly together. His heart swelled with tenderness, a tenderness he'd never known before.

As the man who'd been sitting next to her got up and left, Hank slid onto the stool he'd vacated. "Angela," he said.

She looked up from her plate, her eyes widening with disbelief. "I don't believe this. What are you doing here?"

"I like to eat with the woman I love," Hank replied, loving the color that jumped onto her cheeks. "Do you realize how often you blush, and how utterly charming it is?"

"You're mad," she replied. "You've gone absolutely bonkers."

"I'm not bonkers, I'm in love," he returned. He twirled around on the stool and faced the other diners. "I'm in love," he yelled, his pronouncement met by startled stares. "I'm in love with the woman sitting next to me, and she won't even give me a chance."

"Honey, if you don't want him, I'll take him," an old woman cackled as she winked at Hank.

"Go on, give him a chance," a man at one of the booths bellowed.

Angela bolted from the counter and ran for the door. "Hey," the waitress yelled after her. "You aren't stiffing me."

Hank pulled a handful of bills out of his pocket and threw them on the counter, then raced after Angela. "Angela...wait!"

He couldn't believe how fast she could move. He had to break into a run to catch up with her. "Angela...please." He grabbed her arm. She jerked away from him, then turned to face him.

"Hank, I don't know why you're playing this game, but it isn't going to work." He saw a glimmer of tears in her eyes and instantly regretted his impulsive actions.

"I'm sorry if I embarrassed you," he said softly. "I just thought maybe you'd believe me if I said it out loud in front of other people."

"You did embarrass me. I was mortified," she said, swiping at an errant tear that raced down her cheek.

"That's the last thing I wanted to do," Hank said, kicking himself for his insensitivity. As she started to walk again, he fell into step beside her, his mind racing to find something...anything that would convince her that his love was true.

"Angela...I know I lied to Brody, but I'm not lying now."

"You not only lied about being married to me, you told them I was pregnant," she accused.

"And I think we should stay together for the sake of the baby," he teased. His heart broke when he saw no resulting glint of humor in her eyes. "I'll tell Brody the truth, if that's what it takes to make you believe me."

"Don't be ridiculous," she scoffed. "I don't want you jeopardizing an account." As they reached the office door, she turned and looked at him, her eyes holding an emotion he couldn't discern...maybe regret...sadness...a mixture of both? He couldn't read her, but he knew that the look in her eyes wasn't happiness or joy or belief in his love.

"All I want you to do is let me do my job for the next two weeks, then let me leave. Don't tell me you love me. Don't beg me to stay. It's time for me to move on, and nothing you can say will change my decision."

Hank didn't know what to say. He didn't want to let her go. He didn't want to abide by her decision. But, he also didn't want to make her unhappy.

He sighed and raked a hand through his hair, unsure what to do. "Okay," he agreed. "We'll go back into the office and I'll let you do your job. I won't tell you again that I love you for the rest of the day.''

He saw her visible relief. He unlocked the office door and held it open for her, then added, ''But just for today. I can't make any promises about tomorrow.''

Hank kept his promise for the remainder of the day. After being out of the office for a week, he had a lot of catching up to do and spent the remainder of the morning returning phone calls.

It was just after noon when Angela used the intercom to tell him Sheila was on line one. Instead of taking the call in his office, Hank went out to Angela's desk and picked up the receiver of her phone.

''Did my sweet Hank miss his little Sheila?'' Sheila's baby voice oozed over the line.

''Actually Sheila, I'd like you to be one of the first to know. The most wonderful, crazy, exciting thing happened to me over the past week.'' Hank kept his gaze fixed on Angela. ''I fell head over heels in love with a wonderful woman this past week.'' Angela's eyes widened in horror at the same moment Sheila slammed down her end of the phone. ''Hello? Hello?'' Hank dropped the phone back in its cradle. ''Hmm, guess she didn't want to talk about it.''

Angela grabbed up the phone and held it out to him. ''Call her back,'' she said wildly. ''I can't believe you just did that. Call her back and tell her it was a big joke.''

Hank took the receiver from her and put it in place again. "I won't do that. It's not a joke." He looked at her for a long moment, wanting to say more, but remembering his earlier promise. Without saying another word, he turned and went back into his office.

He walked over to his window and stared outside unseeing. His mind filled with the words Sheila had flung at him the last time they had been together.

She'd warned him that one of these days he would give his heart to a woman and Sheila hoped that woman took it and smashed it into tiny pieces, or something to that effect.

Had Sheila jinxed him? Had she prophesied the doom of his love for Angela? He shoved his hands into his pockets, wondering if Angela would prove to be the one woman in the world he wanted, needed, and the last woman in the world who would love him back.

He closed his eyes, remembering the sweet taste of her kisses, the musical ring of her laughter. What would it take to convince her that his love was real, and not some machination to keep her working for him?

When a woman had seen you lie your pants off, how did you make her realize when you were telling the truth? Unfortunately, he didn't have the answer.

"Mr. Riverton?" Angela's voice came across the intercom. "Jess Maxwell is here to see you."

Jess Maxwell. A potential new client. Hank

pulled his hands from his pockets and buttoned his jacket. He returned to his desk and hit his intercom button. "Send him right in. And Angela, set me up for tomorrow with some interviews for the position of secretary."

He smiled in satisfaction. Maybe the way to make her understand that he didn't care about having her in his life as his secretary was to hire a new secretary, then she couldn't accuse him of using his love to keep her working for him.

His office door opened and a well-dressed young man stepped in. "Mr. Maxwell, nice to see you," he said as he gripped the man's hand in a firm shake.

For the next two hours, Hank and Jess Maxwell conducted business, culminating in Hank gaining the Maxwell account. At the conclusion of their business, Hank walked Jess out, then slapped a folder down on Angela's desk.

"What's that?" she asked warily.

"The details of the Maxwell Skywriter business. I just got the account and Jess Maxwell has a lot of money to burn and a desire to pull out all the stops on an ad campaign."

"So what do you want me to do with this?" She gestured to the folder.

"Take it home and work up some ideas. You said you wanted to be more involved in the creative process of the business…here's your chance."

She frowned and fingered the edge of the manila folder. "This isn't going to change anything,

Hank.'' She stared down, refusing to meet his gaze. ''I've made up my mind, I'm leaving and nothing you do is going to change that fact.''

Hank frowned, again a desperation clawing at his stomach, shooting through his veins. Was she so unaffected by their shared week? Had she not felt the magic when they touched, as they kissed? Could she be so immune to how right it had been when they'd shared their memories and thoughts, their past sadness, their future dreams?

He'd made her a promise. He wouldn't again tell her that he loved her. But he hadn't promised that he wouldn't touch her.

He reached out and tipped her chin, forcing her to look at him. And for a fleeting moment, he saw something in her eyes that gave him hope, a shimmering of emotion that she quickly hid by jerking away from him and standing.

''I'm going home.'' She picked up the folder and her purse. ''I'll work up some ideas for the Maxwell account this evening and bring them in tomorrow morning.'' Again her gaze refused to meet his. ''I've also set up three interviews with potential secretaries first thing in the morning.'' She moved out from her desk and stepped toward the door. ''I'll see you in the morning,'' she said.

Hank nodded. ''Angela.'' He stopped her as she grabbed the doorknob to leave. She turned back to face him. ''I'm not giving up.'' His voice was soft, but rang with determination.

Her cheeks flamed red and she disappeared out

the door. Hank stared after her, his mind racing with options. There had to be some way to convince her his love was true...right. Loving Angela was the first right thing he'd done in a very long time.

The roses had been stupid. She'd ordered so many roses for so many other women, he should have known that the sweet-smelling blossoms wouldn't accomplish anything where her heart was concerned. She was an extraordinary woman, and he needed something inspired to win her heart.

All night he thought of ways to convince Angela he loved her. If he truly believed she felt nothing for him, cared nothing for him, he'd leave her alone. His heart would ache, and he had a feeling Angela was the woman he would never, ever get over. But if she wanted him to, he'd walk away from her and hope eventually she found the man of her dreams.

But he didn't believe she was uncaring or unresponsive to him. She'd been a willing participant in kissing him, in almost making love with him. It had only been her fear and inexperience that had made her call a halt to his caresses.

Yes, he believed he had a tiny piece of her heart. All he had to figure out was how to make her heart completely his.

Chapter Ten

The phone rang just after seven the next morning. Angela jumped up from the table where she'd been having coffee, and quickly picked up, hoping the jangling noise hadn't awakened her mother or her brother.

"Good morning." Hank's deep voice washed over her like a blanket of warmth. She steeled herself against the compelling emotion just the sound of his voice evoked in her.

"What can I do for you?" she asked, keeping her own voice cool and crisp with a slight edge of irritation.

"It's a beautiful morning. The sky is so bright and blue…a perfect background for a message of love. I'll see you in the office at nine."

He clicked off, leaving Angela to stare at the receiver in bewilderment. What was that all about? She hung up and frowned thoughtfully. A message of love? The beautiful blue sky?

She tied her robe more firmly around her waist, her heart beating wildly as she walked to the front door and stepped out into the morning air.

Hank was right. It was a beautiful morning. The scent of fresh morning dew still hung heavy in the air, although the sun had already climbed well above the horizon and the sky was a picture-perfect background for the plane that zoomed across it, spilling smoke in the shape of letters.

"Oh no," she whispered as the first of the sky letters became apparent. She watched in horror as *A N G E L A* appeared across the sky.

"Angela? Everything all right?"

Angela turned to see her mother staring up at the sky. A moment later the two were joined by Brian. "What's going on?" he asked, then followed their gazes to the sky. "Oh wow, that's so cool."

They watched in silence as the plane finished sending its smoke signal. ANGELA I LOVE YOU, blazed across the sky in letters that appeared a hundred stories high.

Tears burned in Angela's eyes as she stared at Hank's words. Even if this wasn't some sort of ruse to keep her at her job, even if he truly believed himself in love with her, how long could his feelings last? Eventually whatever momentary madness that gripped him would ease and he'd realize he wasn't in love with her.

She couldn't give in. She couldn't allow herself to fall into the fantasy he was trying to create. She wouldn't be able to stand to have Hank and all the happiness his love would bring her, then have it snatched away when reality hit him.

"Gosh Angela, this guy must be crazy about you," Brian exclaimed. He scratched his tousled hair. "Well, I'm going back to bed."

Angela turned to face her mother. Janette eyed her daughter with speculation. "Do you need to talk?"

The tears that Angela felt she'd been holding in for a lifetime released themselves. For a moment Angela couldn't speak, her utter heartbreak clogging her throat, making speech impossible.

Her mother gently took her arm and led her through the house and into the kitchen. She pointed to a chair at the table. "Sit," she said, then grabbed several paper towels and handed them to Angela. She sat down in the chair next to her daughter. "Now, tell me what's going on."

Angela sniffled, trying to stop the tears that seemed to have no end. It was as if she'd unstopped a dam and there was nothing left to stem the flow of tears.

Her mother sat patiently as Angela cried. Occasionally Janette would lean forward and pat Angela's hand.

Finally, the tears stopped enough so Angela could talk. She began by telling her mother about their week in Mustang. Although she didn't mention the fact that she and Hank had shared the same bed, she explained about Barbara's workshops and the closeness that had sprung up between Hank and herself.

"I think I've always been a little bit in love with him," she said as she swiped the last of her tears from her cheeks. "From the very first day I started working with him, I entertained a crazy crush that last week blew all out of control."

Janette frowned. "I must be missing something here. You tell me you love Hank and apparently he arranged the air display a little while ago, which means he loves you. So, what's the problem?"

Angela sighed and looked down at the damp paper towel she'd begun shredding. "First of all, I really don't believe he loves me. I think our week in Mustang has confused him. Secondly, even if he believes he loves me, how long will it last? How long will I have him before he decides to cut and run like..."

"Your father," Janette finished. Once again she reached over and touched Angela's hand. "Oh honey." A deep frown etched in the center of her forehead as she gazed at Angela with eyes of sadness. "Angela, I've watched you over the years, and I should have seen things more clearly, should have said something sooner...when you were younger."

"What are you talking about? Said something sooner about what?" Angela looked at her mother curiously.

Janette directed her attention out the nearby window, but her frown didn't ease at all. "As you know, right after your father left us, I developed a heart condition. What I didn't realize until this very moment was that when your father left us, you developed a condition of the heart."

Angela looked at her mother in bewilderment. "I don't understand…"

"I really didn't see the big picture until right now, but suddenly it's all clear to me."

"Mom, you aren't making any sense," Angela exclaimed.

Janette directed her gaze back at her daughter. "When Brian was little and you were in high school, you used him like a shield against dating. You were always too busy for relationships, choosing to attend a Little League game or a Cub Scout meeting over a date."

"That's not true," Angela protested.

Janette held up a hand to still her. "Then when Brian got too old for you to use, you used your work. In every job you've had, you've volunteered for extra duty, longer hours…making a personal life impossible. And it's because you're afraid."

"That's ridiculous," Angela scoffed. She jumped up from her chair, unable to sit still while her mother dissected her life with the precision instrument of a mother's intuition and wisdom.

"No, it's true. Your father's abandonment left a void in your heart, a hole so deep you've never been able to heal it, and you're frightened of letting another man into your life." Janette sighed once again. "I know about that pain, honey, because I have it, too."

Angela turned her back to her mother and stared out the window, tears blurring her vision as she considered what she'd just been told.

Was it true? Had she been far more scarred by her father's abandonment than she'd realized? Had she used the job of raising Brian as protection against involvement, as armor against hurt?

"Angela." Her mother's voice pulled her from her inner turmoil.

"I know about that pain, about that fear because it's what's kept me alone all these years." Her mother's voice was soft with regret. Angela turned to face her, and Janette continued. "Angela, if you love Hank...and if he says he loves you, then embrace it. Grab on to it and hold it tight. Don't let fear keep you alone all your life. I want more for you than that."

Janette stood. "I'm going to go lie down for a little while. Think about it, Angela. Think long and hard before you throw away what might be a wonderful chance for happiness."

Angela watched her mother leave the kitchen, her mind whirling with chaos. She sank back down at the table, her mother's words echoing over and over again in her head.

Grab on to it, embrace it. Oh, how Angela would love to do that. How she would love to get lost in

Hank's love, to dwell in the fantasy his words of love built in her head, in her heart.

Her mother was right. She was afraid. But it was a fear that went deeper than her mother knew. It was not only the fear of abandonment, but the fear of inadequacy, the knowledge that she could never really measure up to what Hank wanted in a woman.

Her mother would never understand that particular fear and it was something Angela was reluctant to tell anyone else. She knew her mother would discount it, would tell Angela how beautiful she was, how special. But, Angela knew the truth. She was...and always would be "funny face."

At a few minutes after eight, Angela called the office and left a message on the machine that she would not be coming into work that day. With Hank's excessive, lavish proclamation of love still burning in her head, she felt far too vulnerable to face him in person.

At nine Brian left for school and her mother dressed and headed out for a doctor's appointment and lunch with friends, leaving Angela alone in the house with only her thoughts for uneasy company.

Always, when Angela didn't want to think, she worked. She spent the morning cleaning the living room, trying not to think of what Hank might be doing, how the interviews for a new secretary were going or why he hadn't called her after the sky message had been sent.

Maybe one of the prospective secretaries was a

gorgeous, big-bosomed blonde who was also bright, efficient and energetic. Maybe the prospective new girl on the block had made him forget all about his "love" for Angela.

It was almost two when she sat down at the kitchen table with the Maxwell folder in front of her. Work. Anything to keep her mind off Hank. She had worked on several ideas for the account the night before, wanting to knock Hank's socks off before she left his firm…his life for good.

Despite the fact that she didn't want to hear from him, the silence of her phone aggravated her. If he loved her so much, why hadn't he called?

At four the doorbell rang and Angela opened the door to see Hank. Standing just behind him was Brody Robinson, who cast her a pleasant, but bewildered smile.

"Hank…what are you doing?" she asked warily.

"That's what I've been asking him for the last three hours," Brody exclaimed. "He tore into Mustang earlier this morning, told me I had to follow him up here, that he had something important he had to tell me, but he had to do it here with you."

"Hank…don't be crazy," she said, her heart thudding rapidly. Surely he didn't intend to do what she thought he did…tell Brody the truth.

"I am crazy," he replied. "Crazed with the need to make you understand my love for you." He turned to Brody. "Brody, I have something to tell you and it isn't something I'm proud of. I lied to you."

Brody's expression of perplexion changed to a frown. "You lied to me? Lied about what?"

"Me and Angela...we aren't married. We pretended to be married because I thought you'd pull your account if you thought I was single."

"Then who is she?" Brody pointed to Angela.

"That's my secretary."

Brody's eyes widened. "You got your secretary pregnant?"

"No!" Hank and Angela's protest rang out in unison.

Brody swiped a hand across the lower half of his face and Hank hurriedly continued to explain. "I talked Angela into pretending to be my wife, but now I've fallen in love with her and want to marry her and she doesn't believe me because I lied to you."

Brody frowned. "Is your name really Angela?" he asked, as if needing some modicum of truth to hang on to.

Angela nodded, her stomach churning with anxiety. The fool. The crazy fool. He shouldn't have done this. He shouldn't have risked the Robinson account to prove a point she would never believe.

Brody drew a deep breath and eyed Hank. "Look, I don't know what's going on between the two of you. I wanted you to have the benefit of Barbara's teachings because I like you. You should have been honest with me from the very beginning."

Hank nodded, regret darkening his eyes. "I know

that now...and if you decide to pull your account from my firm, I'll understand.''

"Pull my account?" Brody looked at Hank as if he had lost his mind. "Hank, I'm a simple man. I love home, hearth and family, but business is business. You're the best damn ad man around. Why in the hell would I want to pull my account?"

He shook his head and pulled the keys to his car out of his pocket. "I don't know what's going on between the two of you. I've never seen two people who looked and acted as married as the two of you did last week."

He looked at Angela. "If you're smart, honey, you'll marry him and put him out of his misery. I've never seen a man as wild-eyed as he was when he showed up at my house earlier today. He went to a lot of trouble to get me here and straighten something the hell out...although I must confess I'm as confused as ever." He shrugged. "I'm going back to Mustang, where my wife is my wife and I know where things stand." He turned and walked to the curb where his car was parked right behind Hank's.

"You crazy fool," Angela said, remembering what he'd said that last night in Mustang. "You went to a lot of trouble to prove a point that wasn't a point at all." Her defenses were back firmly in place.

"What do you mean?" He looked at her in genuine bewilderment.

"You told me you realized the company was

firm financially, that it wouldn't have mattered if you'd lost the Robinson account,'' she replied, desperately guarding her heart against his handsome presence.

He stared at her for a long moment. ''Take a ride with me, Angela.''

''What?'' His sudden shift in conversation confused her.

''Come on. Just take a ride with me. There's something I want to show you.'' He reached out a hand toward her.

''What do you want to show me, Hank?'' She wanted to scream at him, stomp her feet and beg him to go away. She wanted to fling herself in his arms and beg him to hold her tight, tight enough for a single embrace to be enough to last her a lifetime.

''Just please come with me.'' His eyes held a soft vulnerability that pierced through every defense she'd tried to erect against him.

Despite her resolve to the contrary, she placed her hand in his and allowed him to pull her toward his car. She knew she was crazy to spend a minute, a second in his presence. The talk with her mother had left her confused, weak and vulnerable and the last thing she wanted was to fall prey to his fantasy of love for her.

She got into the passenger seat, grateful that the warmth of his hand no longer enclosed hers. As she waited for him to get into the driver's seat, she summoned her strength, sensing she would need all she could muster for whatever new assault he had in mind.

He slid behind the wheel, smiled at her, then started the engine and pulled away from the curb. "Did you get my message this morning?" he asked once they were on the freeway heading out of town.

"You mean that excessive display of nonsense?" she said. She knew she was being mean, but she didn't know how else to keep her emotional distance.

He winced. "Ouch."

"Where are we going?" she asked, then continued before he could reply. "It doesn't matter where you take me, Hank. You could fly me to the moon and it won't make any difference."

"Indulge me, Angela," he said softly. "Perhaps my previous attempts have been extravagant and excessive, but this is the first time I've been so much in love and I don't know the rules."

Angela turned her head and stared out the passenger window so he wouldn't see the aching tears that burned at her eyes. She should have slammed her door in his face. She should have never allowed him to get her into the car. A break was coming, an emotional breakdown she knew would only embarrass herself and probably him as well.

They drove in silence, her refusing to look at anything but the passing scenery, and him concentrating on maneuvering through the rush-hour traffic.

After about fifteen minutes he exited off on a

road Angela had never been on. After a right turn, then a left, they turned onto a dirt road that appeared to lead to nowhere.

Angela shifted in her seat, trying to imagine what insane stunt he intended to pull next. A field with her name plowed in the dirt? A building with her name spray painted on the side?

It didn't matter. Nothing mattered. Nothing Hank Riverton said or did would change her mind. She'd never believe he really loved her. She'd never allow herself to hope...to dream, because the reality hurt too badly.

Chapter Eleven

Hank was out of ideas. Courting the women he didn't care about had been easy. Wooing the woman he loved was the most difficult thing he'd ever done.

He'd spent the entire evening the night before with a Realtor. It was as if all the stars of his fortune had aligned themselves in good luck. The moment Hank had seen the third piece of property the Realtor showed him, he knew it was the place of his dreams, the enchanted land that held his future. Now all he had to do was convince Angela that she was a part of that future.

He looked over at her, his heart thudding so loudly he wondered if she could hear. His palms were damp on the steering wheel. Instinctively he knew he was at the end of the line, that either she loved him or she didn't, that if she denied him this final declaration, he would have to find a way to live without her. And that thought truly terrified him.

He remembered her laughing and telling him he was never alone, implying that he always had some gorgeous woman on his arm for company. But he hadn't lied to her when he'd told her he felt alone. Every day of his life he'd felt alone until that week with her.

Now that he had her so firmly in his heart, he couldn't imagine living the rest of his life without her. Within minutes they'd be at the place where he intended to spend his future. He couldn't imagine her not being there to share that future with him.

He didn't say a word as he turned down the dirt lane that led to the ranch house. In the distance, a gray, weathered barn rose, topped by a copper weathervane. He pulled to a stop in front of the house, shut off the engine, then turned to look at Angela.

She stared out the windshield at the house, her features expressing absolutely no emotion whatsoever.

"It's what we talked about that last night in Mustang," he began, wondering if she could hear his words over the frantic pounding of his heart. "A nice little ranch house with small acreage, a barn for a couple of horses, and a white fenced yard. All it lacks is the flowers you'll plant."

"Why are you doing this?" She finally looked

at him, her beautiful brown eyes awash with tears. "Why are you torturing me this way?" She opened the door and stumbled from the car.

Hank got out of the car and walked to where she stood, her gaze focused on the house while tears slowly coursed down her cheeks.

Her tears were his pain. She didn't want him. She didn't love him. If she did, she wouldn't find his words of love such torture, she wouldn't be so unhappy.

He walked up to the house and sat on the porch, facing where she stood. Drawing a deep breath, he raked a hand through his hair, a dull, hollow emptiness echoing in his heart. "I don't know what to do," he finally said. He knew the abyss of his heart showed in his eyes, it was impossible for such an ache not to show. "I don't know how else to make you understand how much I need you, how much I love you."

The hurt he'd felt when Sarah had left him had been nothing compared to the pain that ripped through him as Angela remained standing where she was, her tears testimony to an unhappiness that could only bode ill for him.

"Tell me you don't care about me, Angela, and I'll leave you alone." He stood and walked to her, stopping only when he was mere inches away from her. His impulse was to take her in his arms, hold her against his heart so she could hear the love that beat with every pulse.

But, he didn't touch her. "Tell me that you don't

feel anything for me and I won't bother you again. But you have to look me in the eyes and tell me that you want me to go away. You need to look me in the eyes and tell me there's no hope." His voice broke as he whispered the last sentence.

She closed her eyes, tears seeping from beneath her eyelids. She drew a deep, shuddery breath, then opened her eyes and met his gaze. "Hank, that week in Mustang was magic...but it was all pretend." She swiped her tears away and straightened her shoulders. "Nothing was real that week and what you're feeling now isn't real."

Hank no longer fought his need to touch her. He grabbed her shoulders, an edge of anger rising up inside him. "Don't tell me what I'm feeling isn't real. I know what's in my heart and I know the difference between real and pretend."

His anger seeped away as unbearable pain tore through him. "I love you, Angela. I want to wake up each morning with you in my arms, and go to sleep at night knowing you're sleeping next to me. Now tell me you don't want me. Tell me you don't care about me."

Angela shoved away from him. "I can't tell you that. Don't you understand anything? I can't tell you I don't care about you. I can't tell you I don't love you."

Her words sang through him, but he still saw no happiness shining from her eyes, no anticipation of a future shared. He placed his palms on either side of her face, wondering what was going on in her

head. What barrier still kept him out of her heart?
"Talk to me, sweetheart. Tell me what's wrong…
tell me why you're crying."

"I'm afraid." The words fell from her lips as if
torn from someplace deep within her.

"Afraid of what?" he asked. With his thumbs he
gently wiped her tears.

Once again she stepped away from him. She
wrapped her arms around herself as if creating a
physical barrier against him…or an enclosure of
self-protection. "I've only loved one man in my
life, Hank, and he walked out of my life without a
backward glance. I couldn't stand it if I gave you
my heart and after a while you gave it back to me."

"Oh Angela." Hank's heart ached for her. "If I
could, I'd go back in time and I'd be your father
and fill the void he left when he walked out on you.
But I can't be your father…I can only be the man
who loves you, who will love you for the rest of
your life."

"But, that's not possible," she exclaimed.
"I'm…I'm not pretty. You can't love me…not really."

Hank stared at her in utter amazement. "Who on
earth ever told you that you weren't pretty?"

"My father."

Hank drew in another deep breath, wondering
how it was possible to despise a man he'd never
met. "Come here," he said and held out his hand
to Angela. "Come on," he urged gently. "Let's sit
down on the porch and talk."

She hesitated a moment, her brown eyes seeking his for some sort of assurance. He nodded, smiled and she placed her hand in his. Together they walked back to the front of the house and sat down side by side on the porch.

"Now, tell me when you had this enlightening conversation with your father," Hank said, refusing to release her hand.

Her cheeks blushed and Hank knew he would do anything to see that this woman was never again hurt by anyone. "It was right before he left us," she began, her voice a whisper of remembered pain. "He told me I'd never be able to depend on my looks, so I'd better be smart." Her gaze was directed to a distant field, as if looking at him while she spoke her father's words would be too painful.

"Now let me tell you something, Angela Samuels," Hank said. He used two fingers beneath her chin to move her head so she had to look at him. "That means you were what, eight or nine, when he said that to you?"

She hesitated, then nodded.

"Honey, I've never seen a nine-year-old girl who I thought might grow up to be a raving beauty. How could your father know, how could he see into the future to know what you would look like at twenty-eight years old?"

"But…"

Hank touched a finger to her lips to still whatever protest she might have launched. "How could he have known that those caramel-colored eyes of yours would shine with such splendor? How would he know that your smile could light up a room, fill the universe with warmth?''

He stroked a finger down the silky skin of her cheek. ''How could a man callous enough to leave his children behind and never look back, know what real beauty is?''

He saw the result of his words getting through, saw it in her small intake of breath, the slight relaxation of her body so close to his. It was a small crack in the armor she wore around her heart.

''Angela, I love you. And when I look at you, my heart beats faster, my pulse races, warmth fills me up. You are more beautiful than you'll ever know…because you're the woman I love.''

A sob escaped her, a sob not of tremendous pain, but rather the sound of pain letting go…giving way and allowing space for a new emotion to appear. ''I love you, Hank.''

His heart, the very spirit that kept him alive, soared with joy at her words. Amazing that those words alone were enough to make him believe anything was possible, to believe that he'd been gifted with the most precious treasure on earth.

He stood, and pulled her up with him. He held back nothing as he wrapped his arms around her, pulled her to him in an embrace. ''I love you, Angela. Marry me. Be my wife. Share my life with me here, in this house.''

She started crying again, but this time he knew the tears did not come from sadness, but rather the happiness of a woman growing sure of the love of her man. "Yes," she managed to say. "Yes, I want that…"

She had no opportunity to say more, for Hank couldn't wait another minute to claim her lips with his. He kissed her, long and deep, sealing their future together with the promise of love forever more.

When he ended the kiss, she touched his face lovingly. "I think I fell in love with you on the first day I met you…that first day I interviewed for the job as your secretary." Her eyes widened and she stepped back from him. "Hank…what about the interviews today. If you drove to Mustang, then you couldn't have interviewed for a new secretary."

"Don't worry about it," he said as he once again drew her close. "Secretaries come and go. I can always hire a new secretary…but wives…now that's a different story altogether. I make you a vow right now, you're the only wife I'm going to have for the rest of my life."

As she gazed at him, the golden light of love flowing from her eyes, bathing him in warmth, he knew he would love her, this woman, his former secretary, his life…until the end of time.

Epilogue

Angela stood staring in the dresser mirror in the bedroom where she and Hank had shared their week of pretend marriage. Clad in a wedding gown with tiny pearl seed buttons and an overlay of delicate lace, she was a vision from her favorite fantasy. Only this was reality, and in just a few minutes she would become Mrs. Hank Riverton.

She shivered with delight, thinking back over the past four weeks. It had been a month since she and Hank had stood before the ranch house and proclaimed their love for one another.

The past thirty days had been a whirlwind of excitement as they prepared for a wedding that would make them the married couple they had once pretended to be. It had been Brody's idea that they wed in the library where they had attended Bar-

bara's marital enrichment workshops. Hank and
Angela had agreed, deciding a small, intimate ceremony was exactly what they wanted.

Throughout the last couple of weeks, Angela's
love for Hank had grown with each day that passed.
They spent every spare moment of every day together, working on ad campaigns, planning their future together and getting the ranch house ready for
their occupancy.

She turned from the mirror as her mother entered
the bedroom. Janette's smile was filled with love as
she gazed at her daughter. "You are absolutely
stunning," she said.

Angela blushed, then took one last look in the
mirror. "I'll do," she said simply.

In Hank's love, he had given her the greatest gift
of all...the ability to look at herself in a mirror, to
accept her strengths and acknowledge her weaknesses. He'd made her realize that beauty had nothing to do with physical features, but rather came
from a place in the heart. And her heart was filled
with it.

"They sent me up to tell you it's time," Janette
said. She walked over and kissed Angela on the
cheek. "I'm so happy for you, Angela. This is one
of the happiest days of my life."

Angela hugged her mother tightly. "I love you,
Mom."

"And I love you, but there's a man downstairs
who has been pacing the length of the floors for the

last fifteen minutes, eager to show you just how much he loves you.''

''Yes, I'm ready.'' Angela smoothed a trembling hand down her dress.

Angela and her mother left the bedroom. Janette preceded her daughter down the wide staircase. As they got to the bottom of the stairs and approached the library door, all the lights in the house went off.

''Mom?''

''It's all right, honey,'' her mother assured her as she pulled open the doors to the library.

Angela caught her breath at the sight that greeted her. Candles. Hundreds of them lit the room, and the scent of orange blossoms wafted in the air.

Candles and orange blossoms. She remembered the day she and Hank had been driving to Mustang for the very first time and they'd discussed the wedding ceremony they'd supposedly shared. The scene in front of her was exactly like she'd described to him on that day. He'd remembered.

He stood by the stone fireplace, looking achingly handsome in a black tuxedo with a pale pink cummerbund and bow tie. He'd remembered it all, and her heart expanded with the wealth of love that flowed through her.

Angela walked toward him, drawn by her love and by the love that shone from his eyes as he looked at her. This man loved her, and she knew in her heart he would never leave her. What they had found together was special...the magic that happens when everything is right.

"You two aren't pulling anything over my eyes this time," Brody's voice boomed out. He pointed to the minister waiting next to Hank. "I checked that man's credentials. He's a real preacher and this is going to be a real wedding." He grinned first at Angela, then at Hank. "And damned if I don't hope we have a real baby within the next year."

Barbara placed a restraining hand on her husband's arm. "Okay, sweetheart, now let's get on with it."

The ceremony passed in a haze. As Hank slipped his mother's ring on Angela's finger, she realized he'd had it sized and it fit perfectly. Like they fit perfectly. As the preacher announced them man and wife, Angela looked into her husband's eyes and knew she was beautiful because she loved and was loved.

*　*　*　*　*

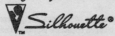

If you enjoyed what you just read,
then we've got an offer you can't resist!

Take 2 bestselling
love stories FREE!

Plus get a FREE surprise gift!

Clip this page and mail it to Silhouette Reader Service™

IN U.S.A.	**IN CANADA**
3010 Walden Ave.	P.O. Box 609
P.O. Box 1867	Fort Erie, Ontario
Buffalo, N.Y. 14240-1867	L2A 5X3

YES! Please send me 2 free Silhouette Romance® novels and my free surprise gift. Then send me 6 brand-new novels every month, which I will receive months before they're available in stores. In the U.S.A., bill me at the bargain price of $2.90 plus 25¢ delivery per book and applicable sales tax, if any*. In Canada, bill me at the bargain price of $3.25 plus 25¢ delivery per book and applicable taxes**. That's the complete price and a savings of over 10% off the cover prices—what a great deal! I understand that accepting the 2 free books and gift places me under no obligation ever to buy any books. I can always return a shipment and cancel at any time. Even if I never buy another book from Silhouette, the 2 free books and gift are mine to keep forever. So why not take us up on our invitation. You'll be glad you did!

215 SEN CNE7
315 SEN CNE9

Name	(PLEASE PRINT)	
Address	Apt.#	
City	State/Prov.	Zip/Postal Code

* Terms and prices subject to change without notice. Sales tax applicable in N.Y.
** Canadian residents will be charged applicable provincial taxes and GST.
  All orders subject to approval. Offer limited to one per household.
  ® are registered trademarks of Harlequin Enterprises Limited.

SROM99   ©1998 Harlequin Enterprises Limited

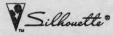

Silhouette ROMANCE™

VIRGIN BRIDES

Your favorite authors tell more heartwarming stories of lovely brides who discover love... for the first time....

July 1999 GLASS SLIPPER BRIDE
Arlene James (SR #1379)
Bodyguard Jack Keller had to protect innocent Jillian Waltham—day and night. But when his assignment became a matter of temporary marriage, would Jack's hardened heart need protection...from Jillian, his glass slipper bride?

September 1999 MARRIED TO THE SHEIK
Carol Grace (SR #1391)
Assistant Emily Claybourne secretly loved her boss, and now Sheik Ben Ali had finally asked her to marry him! But Ben was only interested in a temporary union...until Emily started showing him the joys of marriage—and love....

November 1999 THE PRINCESS AND THE COWBOY
Martha Shields (SR #1403)
When runaway Princess Josephene Francoeur needed a short-term husband, cowboy Buck Buchanan was the perfect choice. But to wed him, Josephene had to tell a *few* white lies, which worked...until "Josie Freeheart" realized she wanted to love her rugged cowboy groom forever!

Available at your favorite retail outlet.

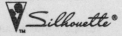

Silhouette®